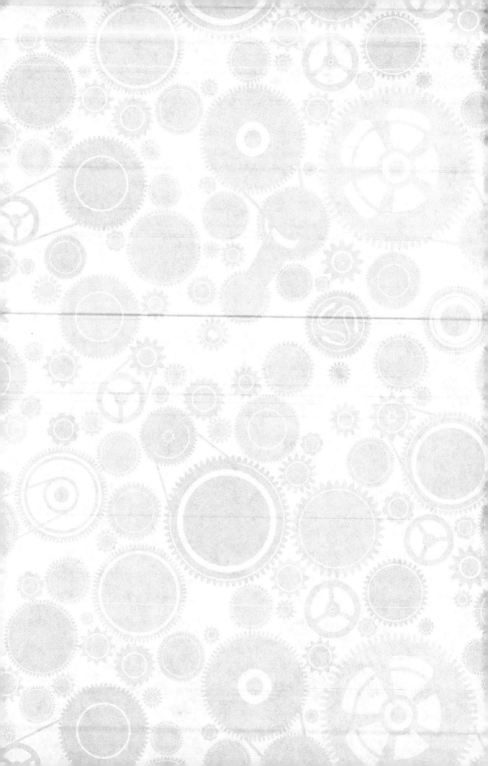

THE BIZARRE BARON INVENTIONS

THE MAGNIFICENT FLYING BARON ESTATE

Eric Bower

Amberjack Publishing
New York, New York

Amberjack Publishing
228 Park Avenue S #89611
New York, NY 10003-1502
http://amberjackpublishing.com

Publisher's Cataloging-in-Publication data
Names: Bower, Eric, author.
Title: The Magnificent flying Baron estate / by Eric Bower.
Description: New York, NY : Amberjack Pub., 2017
Identifiers: ISBN 978-1-944995-13-3 (pbk.) | 978-1-944995-18-8 (ebook) | LCCN 2016954416
Summary: Waldo Baron is dragged into adventure by his inventor parents and a kindly criminal, as they race across the country in the magnificent flying Baron estate!
Subjects: LCSH Flying machines--Juvenile fiction. | Science experiments--Juvenile fiction. | Inventors--Juvenile fiction. | West (U.S.)--History--19th century--Juvenile fiction. | United States--History--19th century--Juvenile fiction. | Adventure fiction. | Humorous stories. | BISAC JUVENILE FICTION / Action & Adventure / General | JUVENILE FICTION / Historical / United States / 19th Century | JUVENILE FICTION / Westerns.
Classification: LCC PZ7.B6752 Ma 2017 | [Fic]--dc23

Cover Design & Illustrations: Agnieszka Grochalska

Printed in the United States of America

For Sebastian

TABLE OF CONTENTS

REAL LIFE IS STRANGER THAN A TALKING SQUIRREL DREAM

JANUARY 25TH, 1891

I had the talking squirrel dream again that night.

And for those of you wondering, yes, it is exactly what it sounds like. In my dream, I'm given a pet squirrel that can talk. I have that dream a lot. I can't really say why. Maybe it's because I'm lonely. Maybe it's because I secretly wish that I had some magic in my life. Or maybe it's because I have a terrible habit of eating beans and hot chilies on fry bread with hard cheese before I go to bed at night. I don't know.

Actually, now that I think about it, it's probably because of the cheese.

Anyway.

In my dream, my Aunt Dorcas comes bursting into my room while I'm reading in my bed.

"Hello there, my little Waldo!" she sings in her high and wobbly voice, knowing full well that I hate my first name more than I hate pickled pig's feet for supper. "Your parents have a little gift for you!"

I roll my eyes as I bury myself underneath my cowboy novel.

"Don't you want to guess what it is?" she sings.

"No."

"Guess anyway!" she sings again.

"Go away."

"I'm going to keep singing until you show some interest in the surprise! Lalalalaaaaaa!! Dooo dee doo dooooo!! Woah woah weee womp woooo!"

Listening to my aunt sing is like being kicked in the head by a bull over and over again. Actually, no, it's worse. The kick would at least knock you unconscious. With Aunt Dorcas, you're forced to listen to her dreadful voice until you either run away or stuff your ears with mashed potatoes.

"This is torture, Aunt Dorcas!"

"Womp womp beee boooooo!" she continues to sing.

I can't take it anymore.

"Okay, fine, you win. Please stop," I say. "What is it? What's the surprise?"

"It's a present from your parents for your birthday!" she sings.

She presents me with a little cage that has a sheet draped over it. I slowly get out of bed and put my cowboy novel on my nightstand. I pull the sheet away, and I see a squirrel sitting in the cage. It's a little, grey squirrel with a puffy tail. Aside from the fact that it's wearing tiny, oval-shaped reading glasses and a miniature white coat, it looks like a perfectly ordinary squirrel.

"My parents got me a squirrel for my birthday," I say, shaking my head in disbelief. "Three years ago, I asked them for a dog for my birthday, and they gave me a plant. Two years ago, I asked for a bow and arrow set, and so they gave me new shoes. This year, I asked for a book, and they gave me a squirrel. They always give me the opposite of what I ask for."

"How is a book the opposite of a squirrel?" Aunt Dorcas asks.

"I don't know. It just is."

Here is where the dream gets weird . . .

"Happy birthday, W.B.," says the squirrel in my father's

voice.

I'm so shocked that the squirrel has spoken that I drop its cage onto the floor.

"Ouch!" the squirrel cries, rubbing its little backside. "W.B., please be more careful! My bones are much more delicate now that I have a squirrel body."

"P?" I gasp. "Is that really you?"

I call my parents P and M instead of Pa and Ma. And they call me W.B. instead of Waldo Baron. We all sort of prefer it that way. The only person who goes by their regular name is Aunt Dorcas, which is odd, because she has the worst name out of all of us.

My father, the squirrel, begins to explain to me how he and my mother have just completed another successful experiment which allowed them to place their minds into the bodies of other creatures.

"Don't you see what this means?" my little squirrel-father says, hopping up and down with excitement. "It means if you've ever wanted to fly, you can place your mind into the body of a bird! If you want to swim under the sea, you can place your mind into the body of a fish! This is the greatest scientific breakthrough in history! In history! I'm so excited!"

"Would you like an acorn?" I ask with a grin.

"OH MY GOODNESS, I WOULD LOVE AN ACORN! GIVE ME A—wait, stop that!" my father says, blushing beneath his squirrel beard. "You're not taking this seriously, W.B. That's your biggest problem. You don't take science seriously."

He's probably right. But he's also a squirrel, which makes it rather hard to take *him* seriously.

"If you could put your mind into the body of any animal in the world, why did you choose a squirrel?" I ask. "I thought you hated squirrels."

"A squirrel is the only animal I could catch. And I don't hate them," my father replies defensively, twitching his little nose and stroking his puffy tail. "I just hate when they get into the garage and chew on my experiments. You used to do the same thing when you were an infant. You always chewed and drooled on everything. At times you seemed more like a camel than a baby."

"Will you be able to put your mind back into your body?" I ask. "Actually . . . where is your body?"

It's rather creepy to think of my father's body sitting around his work garage without a mind in it.

"Oh, your mother is watching it," he tells me. "She has to. Otherwise it might get into trouble."

"How can your body get into trouble without a mind in it?"

"It does have a mind in it," my squirrel father explains. "I didn't get rid of the squirrel's brain. That would be cruel. So I simply switched it with mine. My body currently has a squirrel brain in it. Now that I've shown you what your mother and I have been working on, I'm going to go switch back. Would you please let me out of my cage?"

I open the cage and my swift, little squirrel-father bolts out of it and heads towards the door. The moment he reaches it, he bumps into an excited, little prairie dog. The prairie dog is also wearing little spectacles and a coat.

"Isn't this fantastic!" says the prairie dog in my mother's voice. "I feel stronger and quicker than I have in years! I think I can even do a cartwheel. Watch me a do a cartwheel!"

"Sharon!" my squirrel father squeaks. "I told you to wait until I was human again before switching your brain with the prairie dog!"

Which is quite possibly the weirdest

sentence a son will ever hear his father say.

"I couldn't wait!" my prairie dog mother says, spinning around and hunching over in her furry little body. "It was too exciting!"

"But . . . Sharon," my squirrel father says desperately, "don't you see what this means?"

Before my squirrel father can explain what it means, we hear a terrible thundering noise.

The bodies of P and M—now with the brains of a terrified squirrel and a baffled prairie dog—come tearing down the hall. They are squeaking and shrieking and looking for the nearest tree to climb.

And that's when I always wake up.

I wake up in a cold sweat, usually with a cowboy novel on my chest and a bellyache from my late night snack. I'm terrified, but after a few deep breaths, I look around my bedroom, and I realize that everything is alright. My parents are not squirrels or prairie dogs. Their weird, scientific-inventor brains are still in their weird, scientific-inventor bodies. My Aunt Dorcas is still annoying and sings all the time, but that's alright. I suppose.

Everything is normal, or, at least as normal as it can be here at the Baron Estate, which is the name of our home. The Baron Estate is located just a few miles outside of the town of Pitchfork, which is in the heart of Arizona Territory. Pitchfork is one of the wilder towns in the new American frontier, which I like. It's also one of the hottest, which I don't like. I suppose you could say I'm sort of a heavyset kid, so I don't do very well in the heat.

When I wake up in the morning, I like to look out the window at the quiet desert that surrounds our home and dream about the heroic gunfights that are happening over in Pitchfork. There's a legendary sheriff there by the name of Sheriff Hoyt Graham, who is said to be one of the bravest men in the world. He singlehandedly captured a gang of fifty armed bandits, led by the dastardly bank robber, Benedict Blackwood. No one had ever been able to capture Benedict Blackwood before, but Sheriff Hoyt Graham had made it look easy. There have been hundreds of short stories and novels written about Sheriff Graham's adventures, and I've read each and every one of them. Even though it makes me sound like a bad person, there are times when I wish I was his kid instead of M and P's. At least Sheriff Graham makes sense to me.

On that particular morning, I was feeling excited

because I suddenly remembered what was happening in Pitchfork later that day. Sheriff Hoyt Graham and his deputies were going to put on a show for everyone in town with wild stunts and rope and horse tricks. The sheriff was also going to tell the crowd about some of his greatest adventures, including the ones that haven't been written in books yet. I'd been looking forward to seeing him for months.

But on that very morning, when I looked out my bedroom window, I did not see the quiet desert or the hills that lead to Pitchfork. In fact, I saw nothing but blue. Blue and more blue, surrounding a lot of bluish blue with bluey blueness. I rubbed my eyes and pinched myself to make sure that I wasn't still dreaming.

I stuck my head all the way out the window, looked down, and gasped.

I finally saw the desert. It was hundreds and hundreds of feet below us. The Baron Estate was floating in the sky like a hot air balloon.

"W.B.!" I heard M call from downstairs. "Come here! We've got a wonderful surprise for you!"

I pinched myself again. Nope. Still awake.

It was just one of those times in life when real life is stranger than a talking squirrel dream.

MAGNUS KICKED AUNT DORCAS IN THE KNEE

After recovering from the dizzying sight of the earth being several hundred feet below me, I rushed out of my bedroom and made my way down the staircase. When I reached the living room, I found M, P, and Aunt Dorcas sitting together on the sofa. M was comforting my aunt, who was weeping hysterically. P was unfolding a large blueprint of our home, with a lot of extra squiggles, letters, and numbers written on it.

"What's happening?" I cried. "The house is flying!"

"No, it isn't," my father said, without looking up from his blueprint.

I went to the front door and opened it. I looked down and almost threw up. Our house was now so high up in the sky that I could barely see through the clouds to the ground.

"P . . . I'm pretty sure that we're flying," I said.

"You're wrong."

He went back to his plans, making a note on the blueprint with his fountain pen.

Sometimes he can be a very frustrating man.

I walked over to him and tapped him on the shoulder. He looked up at me.

"Yes?" he asked.

"May I please borrow your pen, P?" I asked.

"Yes, of course."

He handed me the pen. Without a word, I turned and threw it out the open door.

"We are flying," I repeated to my father. "That is why your pen is now falling hundreds and hundreds of feet back to earth. Why are we flying?"

"Oh dear, I hope that pen doesn't hit anyone," M said.

"Goodness!" Aunt Dorcas blubbered.

"We're not *flying*," P repeated, sounding a bit annoyed. "We're *floating*. I've found a way to make our house float, but I'm still trying to figure out a way to control its direction and speed. Since I can't move the house forward or steer it, I hardly think it's fair to describe what the house is doing as *flying*. A hot air balloon *flies* because it can be controlled. But a regular balloon, without any controls, just *floats*. Understand?"

I did understand, but I wished my father wouldn't bother with unnecessary explanations. He knew what I meant.

"Alright . . . why are we *floating*?" I asked, trying very hard to stay calm.

My father opened his mouth to answer me . . . and then stopped. His eyes grew wide from behind his spectacles as he brought his face closer to the blueprint.

"I say . . .," he murmured to himself, lifting his glasses and making a funny face. "What if I . . . yes, yes . . . maybe . . . xylophone? No . . . probably . . . yes . . . but no . . . if I . . . yes! Marmosets? Perhaps . . . kind of . . . but I can't . . . Rutabaga! Yes, I can . . . will I though? Hasenpfeffer . . . hmmmm."

He mashed his index finger and thumb together and began to rub them against the blueprint as though he had forgotten that he was no longer holding his pen. My mother took a pencil from her coat pocket and put it between P's thumb and index finger. He continued writing, this time actually making marks on the blueprint, and then he stopped.

"Hmmm," P said as he stroked his chin, smearing the charcoal from the pencil onto his face. "Sharon? Please take a look at this. I might have just fixed our problem."

"Of course, dear," my mother said, still patting her weeping sister on the back. "W.B.? Would you please take over for me while I help your father?"

I sighed.

I went to the sofa and sat down. As M released Aunt Dorcas, my aunt wrapped her arms around me instead. Someone always had to comfort Aunt Dorcas. She was as fragile as an egg and sort of shaped like one as well.

Come to think of it, she usually smelled like eggs too. Was it possible for a person to be part egg?

"We're flying," Aunt Dorcas cried into my ear in a runny voice. "I hate heights. I hate being up in the air. I hate it, I hate it, I hate it! I hate flying."

"We're not flying," I told her. "We're floating. Apparently there's a big difference."

"I think you've figured it out!" M said to P, giving him a huge hug. "The steam thrusters that we built just needed to be angled. We can do this! We can fly the Baron Estate!"

They both jumped into the air and did the silly dance that they do when they're happy. Have you ever had a bee fly into your trousers? If so, you've probably done my parents' happy dance. I hope they've never done it in public. It's ridiculously embarrassing.

"That's great," I said, unlatching myself from my soft boiled aunt, "but why are you doing this? And when can we go back down to the ground? I have school tomorrow, and I don't think the teacher will believe me if I tell her that I had to miss class because my house was floating."

"Not *floating*," my father corrected with a huge smile on his face. "*Flying*! I've done it! I've discovered how to make the Baron Estate fly! They said it couldn't be done! Hah! Well, I've proven them wrong yet again! Hah! Hah ha! Hahahahaha!"

My father says this often—that he has proven "them" wrong—before bursting into maniacal laughter. But I don't think anyone really knows what he means by it. I've asked him before who "they" are, and why "they" always doubt him, but he's never been able to give me an answer. Frankly, I don't think he knows either. I also don't know why he laughs maniacally after saying it. Sometimes it seems like my father's cheese has slipped off his cracker, if you know what I mean. He's one grape short of a fruit salad, if you catch my drift. His corn hasn't been cut off the cob. His potato was peeled with a dull spoon. Someone let his onion boil for a little too long.

In other words, there's something a little bit wrong with him.

You see, most of the other children I know have parents who are farmers or tailors or butchers or bakers. I'm the only one I know with parents who are inventors. They design and build funny, little gadgets and gizmos. Our house is their playground. The Baron Estate looks like something out of a wild dream, with steaming beakers over open flames in the kitchen, and glass tubes filled with brightly-colored, bubbling liquids flowing from one room to the next, and hundreds of metallic devices with coils and wires and strings and gears that do crazy things like fry an egg, shine your shoes, sweep the floor, and part your hair when you press a single button.

When I wake up in the morning and I see a mechanical butler offering me toast and eggs, or when I walk out the door to see my father traveling across our property on a horseless carriage, or my mother wearing a pair of mechanical arms that have made her strong enough to rip a large tree out of the ground . . . I'm no longer surprised. It's just what everyday life is like here at the Baron Estate. I've only had one kid from school come over to the house, and he ran away screaming. He told all the other kids that I lived inside a crazy windup clock and that my parents were from the planet Mars.

He might be right about my parents—I've actually had the same thought before—but it still wasn't a particularly nice thing to say.

It's not easy having parents who are so different. For one thing, it makes all the other children think I'm different as well, which is why I don't have any friends.

"M?" I asked. "What's P talking about?"

M reached into the pocket of her work coat and handed me a folded up piece of paper. I unfolded it and saw that it was cut out of the science magazine that my parents always buy, *Inventor's Quarterly: The Publication for Serious Inventors.* At the top of the paper was a drawing of a hot air balloon with a large dollar sign on it. It was an advertisement for some sort of a contest.

A CALL TO INVENTORS, INNOVATORS, TINKERERS, ADVENTURERS, AND THOSE

WHO SIMPLY SEEK MONEY, FAME, AND EXCITEMENT!

Hortense's Tooth Power is sponsoring a race around the country for anyone with adventure in their hearts, genius in their brains, moxie in their socks, and gumption in their knees!

Anyone willing to join the fantastic race across the country must bring *their own unique vehicle* (for example—a new kind of high-powered hot air balloon, or a floating carriage, or a flying railroad car, or a land ship, or whatever crazy kind of vehicle your imagination can create!) and meet us at The Grand Exposition Fairgrounds in Chicago, Illinois on January 26th, 1891, no later than noon.

An entry fee of five dollars and twenty-eight cents must be provided. A reminder: all vehicles used by contestants *must* be unique. The first team to complete the race, without breaking any rules or laws, will win $500!!!

"I don't get it," I said.

I actually did get it, but I needed to hear it from one of my parents in order to believe it.

My father, ignoring me as usual, rolled up his blueprint and dashed out of the living room. I knew where he was going. He was going to his work garage, which, fortunately for him, was attached to the side of the Baron Estate. If it were a detached garage, my absentminded father would have probably thrown open the backdoor and stepped outside, plummeting several hundred feet back to earth.

My father, McLaron Baron, is one of the strangest men in the world; he's also probably one of the smartest. His hair is bright white and sticks straight up in the air as though he's just been struck by lightning. It's been that way ever since he was first struck by lightning seven years ago. Since then, he's been struck by lightning nineteen times. It's the darnedest thing. Every time his hair starts to return to its normal color he gets struck by lightning again. M says he must have a metal plate in his head that attracts lightning like a flame attracts a moth. But that's another story . . .

Anyway, P can look at the most complicated machine or device and tell you exactly how it works, and he invents things that are truly amazing. But he often forgets the simplest things, like the name of his son, or where he left his horse—*oh my gosh where did he leave his horse?*—or where his house is located. He's the sort of man who will come up with a brilliant idea while shaving in the morning and rush excitedly out of the house dressed only in his long under-wear. In fact, he's done that twice this month.

"We're going to enter the countrywide race, and we're going to win it," M told me with a grin. "Your father and I have been looking for an excuse to create a unique flying machine. And now we've done it. We're going to enter that contest and win it. We can use that $500 to hire an assistant to help us with our future experiments and inventions. Isn't that exciting?"

"I need some warm milk," bubbled Aunt Dorcas. "This is all very upsetting."

She let go of me and walked through the large double doors that led to the kitchen. My nightshirt was drenched with her yolky tears.

"But what about school?" I said to M.

In all honesty, I couldn't care less about school. I was thinking about Sheriff Graham and his deputies, and how I'd miss the show if I went along on P and M's wacky race around the country.

"I already contacted your schoolteacher," M said as she brushed down the cowlick in my hair. "Miss Danielle believes that it will be a wonderful learning experience for you to travel the country. She expects a full report on it when you return. You'll present it to the entire class. Isn't that exciting?"

I groaned. Miss Danielle was always looking for an excuse to assign one of her students a report to present to the class. Last year a kid had broken his nose badly and needed surgery, and when he came back he was forced to give a report about his surgery with his nose all stuffed up and bandaged. He had spoken to the class for close to an hour, and no one could understand a thing he was saying because his nose was too swollen. Later on, the kid admitted that he hadn't prepared a report and was actually just saying gibberish, which I thought was a brilliant idea.

"Well, I don't see how we can join the race," I said. "It says we have to be in Chicago by the twenty-sixth. We'll never make it there in time."

My mother grinned. There was a glimmer of excitement in her eyes.

Like my father, M also has an odd little brain. She's a mathematical genius who is able to take P's wild ideas and apply some logic to them. They both have the same talent for tinkering, and spend most of their time working together in the workshop in our garage. Unlike the other mothers I know, she can't cook or clean worth a darn, and she doesn't seem to care.

"Let Aunt Dorcas cook dinner and sweep the floors," she told me when I brought the subject up to her. "Or better yet, you can do it yourself, W.B.; I have important things to do."

She also refuses to wear dresses or style her hair like the other mothers. She always wears work clothes and ties her long hair back out of her face with a piece of twine. Her face is often dirty with grease and oil from working on machines. I love her dearly, but I often wonder how a man like P and a woman like M could have a child like me (W.B.). It doesn't seem mathematically possible.

Or maybe it is. To tell you the truth, I'm not very good at math.

"I don't think we'll have a problem getting to Chicago on time. In fact, we're planning on getting there early," she said to me. "W.B., I think you should close the front door and have a seat. Hold on tightly to something, preferably something heavier than you."

Before I could ask her why, the entire house suddenly

jerked to the side, knocking me over and sending me tumbling into the wall. I narrowly missed falling out of the open front door. The framed family portrait my parents had taken last year fell off the wall and bonked me on the head. For a moment I saw funny, little, pink squirrels circling my head—*why is it always squirrels?*

The Baron Estate began to move eastward. It was like our house was being pulled through the sky by a chariot of giant invisible horses. It was incredible. I stuck out my foot and kicked the front door shut.

There was a terrible clatter from the kitchen, the sound of plates, cups, glasses, and silverware all falling to the floor. I heard Aunt Dorcas scream in pain.

My mother rushed into the kitchen to check on her.

I sat there on the floor, leaning against the wall while I watched all of our bookcases, lamps, and furniture slowly swaying as we sailed through the sky. It was the strangest thing I had ever seen, and, considering who my folks are and what they do, that's really saying something. I looked out the window and saw that we were indeed moving much faster than I thought possible. It was fascinating to see the brown, green, blue, and yellow land below; the land that I had never in my wildest dreams imagined I would one day be flying over. We were up so high that I couldn't make out any buildings or towns. It looked as though the world beneath us was completely empty.

My mother stuck her head out of the kitchen.

"W.B., would you please come in here and help? Magnus kicked Aunt Dorcas in the knee."

WHACKED IN THE
BACKSIDE BY OUR GARAGE

Magnus is our horse. It turns out that when my father decided to float the Baron Estate, he brought his horse inside and then forgot that he had left him in the kitchen. Magnus was just as confused as I was about our home finding a new address up in the clouds. Magnus was a very sensible horse. In fact, he was probably the most sensible creature in the Baron Estate. Often, when my father would try to use Magnus in his experiments (like when he placed electric horseshoes on his hooves to make him run faster, or the time he tried to attach a propeller to Magnus's backside to turn him into what he called a *horse-e-copter*), our horse would give him a look that seemed to say, "Are you utterly insane? I am a horse. A horse! Just let me be a horse, for goodness' sake."

After helping Aunt Dorcas with her aching knee and sweeping up all the broken glass and china, M and I joined P in the garage.

P had slipped on a pair of dark goggles and leather gloves. He was steering our home with a large wooden wheel that looked like it belonged on a pirate ship.

It had been a long time since I had set foot in the garage. I typically wasn't allowed in there, and, to be honest, I didn't really care enough about my parents' inventions and experiments to sneak a look inside when they weren't around. My Sheriff Hoyt Graham books were much more interesting to me than a bunch of smoking and buzzing doo-dads or copper and leather gizmos. But the garage had undergone a complete transformation that took my breath away.

In addition to the steering wheel, the entire garage had been redone to resemble the inside of a ship, with a giant compass located beside the wheel, a map of the world pasted onto the ceiling, and the largest spyglass (an interesting invention used by sailors at sea to see things from a great distance) that I had ever seen. The end of the spyglass had been stuck through a hole cut into the wall, and, when I looked through it, I was able to see what was happening on the ground. My parents had added a large picture window to the front of the garage to give them a better view of what was in the sky ahead.

There were also random turning gears and smoking machine parts everywhere and a giant, coal-burning furnace that had been installed in the corner. I thought about the kid who had described our home as the inside of a crazy windup clock. I wondered what he would think about the Baron Estate now . . .

"Welcome to the magnificent flying Baron Estate!" P called to me. "Your mother and I are co-captains of this ship, which means that you are the first mate."

I looked out the window and saw a team of flying ducks gaping at us.

One of them quacked loudly at me. It looked pretty angry. I guess I would be sort of angry too if I came home

one day and found a bunch of ducks sitting in my bedroom where they didn't belong.

I shrugged at the duck and mouthed an apology. The duck rolled its eyes at me before leading the rest of the ducks as far away from the Baron Estate as possible.

"Is this thing safe?" I asked. "Why didn't you tell me that you were doing this to our home? Do you really think you can navigate a house around the country? How long do you think it'll take?"

"You're supposed to say 'aye aye, Captain,' when the captain speaks to you," P replied, completely ignoring my questions.

My mother leaned in and kissed me on top of the head.

"You always have so many silly questions," she said. "Why don't you go and get dressed? We have lots of planning ahead of us, and we'll need our first mate's help."

"But I don't want to be a first mate," I protested.

"Fine, you can be the second mate," M said. "Aunt Dorcas will be the first mate. It's your loss, though, since the first mate gets to wear a nifty hat. Now go get dressed. I don't want you walking around without shoes on. More glass might break, and we don't have time to take you to a doctor if you cut yourself."

I grumbled to myself as I walked out of the garage, down the hallway, and up the stairs back to my bedroom. It was a long walk that required a lot of grumbling. By the time I was dressed and had walked back to the garage, my throat was a bit sore from all my grumbling. But I couldn't help it. I was annoyed at being uprooted from my life and dragged into one of my parents' strange, little projects. I know I should have been amazed that they were able to transform our home into a flying machine, but I was just upset. *Why did they have to do this on today of all days?*

While P was steering the Baron Estate, M was planning our route on the map on the ceiling. To do that, she had taken a long stick and stuck a charcoal pencil to the end of it. She held up her arm and traced the route she thought would be the quickest way for us to get to Chicago.

"We have enough coal to get us there," she was saying, "but we'll need to buy more in Chicago. I've calculated precisely how much coal we'll need to get us around the country. Perhaps we should store the coal in Aunt Dorcas's room. It is the largest room in the house. She won't be happy, but, then again, she's never happy."

"Yes," P agreed. "She's usually unhappy. In fact, she seems to *enjoy* being unhappy. The only time I've ever seen her happy is when she's unhappy. We should try our best to make her as unhappy as possible."

"That's very sweet of you, McLaron."

"Thank you, Sharon."

"Why didn't you just build a hot air balloon?" I interrupted.

They both jumped. When they were having one of their discussions they rarely noticed anyone else existed.

"Pardon me?" M said.

I felt my face begin to turn red with anger.

"A hot air balloon. Or some other flying device. Why did you do this to our home?" I asked. "And more importantly, why didn't you ask me if I wanted to come along?"

P and M both looked confused.

"But . . ." my father began, removing his goggles and cleaning them with his handkerchief, "why *wouldn't* you want to come with us?"

"We thought you'd be thrilled," said M with a frown. "You're always reading about terrific adventures in your books. This is the chance for a real life adventure."

"This is the chance to see things that have yet to be written about in novels," my father told me. "This is your chance to be the one who writes the stories and experiences the excitement instead of just reading about it."

"This is a once in a lifetime opportunity," M continued, "and with the prize money for winning the race, we can finally afford the assistant that we need to take our inventions to the next level. With three inventors working together, we can be so much more successful. We can finally make our dreams come true."

"This is our chance to be a part of history," said P. "And we can do it as a family."

"What do you have to say to that?" M asked.

"Duck," I said.

Both my mother and father ducked their heads.

"No, duck!" I said, pointing out the window. "Straight ahead!"

A lone duck that had become separated from its group

turned around just in time to get whacked in the backside
by our garage.

GET COMFORTABLE
OR GET SHOT

My parents were right. We arrived in Chicago six hours later. I didn't think it would be possible, but when my parents set their minds to something, there is little they can't accomplish.

I was still feeling quite sour because when I glanced at my pocket watch, I saw that the Sheriff Graham show had already started. And I was stuck hundreds of miles away. I had been told by the other children at school that this would likely be the last of his shows, since the sheriff was set to retire soon. *Great. Just great.*

We landed the Baron Estate in the Exposition Fairgrounds of Chicago, and through the windows I could see the ooohing and ahhhing faces of the crowd that had gathered. They ooohed, and then they ahhhed, all at the same time, as though they had practiced it the night before. They were really quite good at it.

There were many fantastic inventions already parked on the fairgrounds. There was a railroad car that was fitted with giant flapping wings, which frequently rose up into the air and belched a dark cloud from its smokestack before landing. There was a large wooden ship with metal wheels on the side that was drawn by two dozen miserable looking buffalo—though now that I think about it, I can't remember the last time I saw a happy buffalo, can you?

Not all of the transportation devices brought by the inventors were large, though. At the far end of the grounds I saw a little, two-seated device with a propeller fastened to the top. Beside the propeller device was a little wheeled glider that could barely fit one tiny person in the driver's seat. To the left of us was a strange invention that looked like a combination between an electric bicycle and a fish. And a funny looking man with a large hat had parked a wagon filled with bananas to the right of us, though he might not have been participating in the race.

On second thought, he was probably just selling bananas.

"Now what?" I asked my parents.

They both yawned and stretched. Aunt Dorcas, who was now hobbling around on crutches and complaining about her cracked knee to anyone who would listen, told me that my parents hadn't slept much in the past few weeks. Their minds were completely focused on transforming the Baron Estate for the national race.

I noticed that she was wearing a nifty, new hat that said "FIRST MATE" across the front.

I'll admit it. I was a bit jealous of the nifty hat.

"Alright, now it's time for sleep," said my father. "The contest doesn't begin until noon tomorrow. I'd like to get at

least 3,114 winks before then.
Sharon?"

"I agree," M yawned.
"If I don't sleep soon,
I'm going to fall
asleep while standing
u—"

She was unable to
finish her sentence before
falling asleep. She often fell asleep
while standing. Once I saw her fall asleep while making a
cheese sandwich, pulling the bread over her shoulders as
though it were a blanket. P threw M over his shoulder as
he made his way to their bedroom at the other end of the
house.

"Are you going to sleep too?" I asked Aunt Dorcas.

"Certainly not," she griped, wincing as she favored her
sore knee. "I've probably shattered every bone in my knee.
I'm disfigured for life. I'll never be the same again. I will
feel this terrible pain for the next thirty-seven-and-a-half
years. I'm probably bleeding from the inside. Does it look
like I'm bleeding from the inside?"

"No."

"Well . . . you're clearly not a doctor!" she cried rottenly, before hobbling away.

I was alone. Everyone had gone to their rooms, leaving me with nothing to do. Since I was in a new city, it made sense that I should do a bit of exploring. I took Magnus by the reins and led him out the front door.

The moment I stepped outside, I was surrounded by a large crowd of reporters who began to ask me questions.

"Hey kid, is this your invention?" a man with a notepad called.

"How did you get your house to float?"

"Can you make my house float too?"

"Is it floating or is it flying? There's a big difference, you know."

"What're you going to do with the money if you win it?"

"Why do you keep your horse inside?"

"Is Hortense's Tooth Powder your favorite brand of tooth powder?"

"Is this the first thing you've ever invented?"

"Who's your favorite inventor?"

"Is it safe to fly a house across the world?"

"What happens if someone tries to send you mail?"

It wasn't just reporters who were interested in the Baron Estate. The other inventors looked fascinated by it as well. They peppered me with questions about the science behind the flying house.

"It's steam powered, isn't it?" an inventor wearing goggles and a long white coat asked me.

"Errr, it's coal powered," I told him.

"What is the airspeed velocity?" another asked.

"Uhhh . . . yes?"

"How do you steer it?"

"With a steering wheel."

"Has anyone seen my hat?" a hatless man asked. "I left it on the ground right there an hour ago."

He pointed towards the Baron Estate.

"Umm, it must have blown away," I told him.

The questions kept coming, most of which I couldn't answer or understand, and so I did what I imagined Sheriff Graham would have done if he had been in my situation. I hopped on my horse and ordered the crowd of reporters and inventors to part and let me pass.

To my surprise, they did.

Huh. I guess I should try ordering people around more often, I thought.

I rode out of the fairgrounds and began to trot down the city street. I had never been to Chicago before. Heck, I had only been out of Arizona Territory once in my life, and that's when I was born, so I don't really remember it too well. I was amazed at how many people there were, moving up and down the busy streets and walking in and out of beautiful, tall buildings, which made me feel very small and insignificant.

As I rode, I felt my stomach begin to rumble. I hadn't eaten since last night, and I was feeling quite hungry. There was food back at home in the pantry, but I didn't feel like going back just yet. I had a bit of money in my pocket, so when I found what looked to be a little restaurant, I tied Magnus's reigns to a hitching post on the corner and went inside.

It was busy with crowds of people laughing, singing, and dancing. There was a man playing a funny song on a piano in the corner. Most of the people were sitting on stools in front of a long wooden counter at the other side of the room. There was an empty stool at the end of the counter, so I hopped up onto it and cleared my throat. A gruff-looking man appeared from behind the counter. He had the largest mustache I had ever seen. It looked like he'd glued two beaver tails to his face.

I leaned forward. Upon closer inspection, I realized that he *had* glued two beaver tails to his face.

"Whadda ya want?" he asked me from beneath his beavery mustache.

"I'm hungry," I told him.

"Well, so am I. What do you want me to do about it, kid?"

He glared at me, pulling a fork from his apron and using it to slowly comb his giant mustache. I noticed that there were several people staring at me. It took me a moment to realize that there weren't any other kids in there.

"Isn't this a restaurant?" I asked meekly.

"The kid thinks this is a restaurant!" one of the men beside me chuckled as he took a large swig from his drink.

"This is a saloon," the falsely mustachioed man told me as he put his fork back into his pocket. "It's for grownups only. No kids allowed. Scram!"

"Yeah, scram, kid!" a man beside me echoed.

"Go back to Mommy and Daddy!" another called out.

"Come back when you don't wear diapers no more!"

Soon, everyone was laughing at me.

I could feel my face turning bright red. I slid off the stool and prepared to slink out of the saloon in shame when, suddenly, I heard a girl's voice cry out.

"Hey! Wait!"

I heard the voice, but I couldn't see the voice's owner because she was standing behind the bar, and she appeared to be incredibly short. The mustachioed man looked down and frowned. At least I assumed he frowned. It was kind of hard to tell because of the giant mustache.

"Yes, sweetheart?" he said, leaning down.

A small hand reached up and grabbed one tail of his fake mustache, yanking him down to the ground. The man cried out in pain as he fell. Everyone in the saloon laughed.

"The boy is hungry," the little voice from behind the counter said. "Make him a cheese sandwich."

"Buh sweeharp," the mustachioed man slurred, his voice sounding strange since his mustache was being pulled, "we duh hab buch cheese! Oww! Ohhh-oww!"

The little hand yanked on the glued mustache even harder.

"Make him a cheese sandwich, or I'll tell Ma you're combing your fake, ratty mustache with one of her good forks again."

"Bine! Bine! I'll bake buh boy a cheese sammich immbebiabely! Immbebiabely!" the man cried, and then the little hand let his beaver tail go.

As the man quickly scurried into the back room to make the cheese sandwich, the little girl hopped onto the counter. Though she was barely over three feet tall, I could tell we were about the same age. She was dressed like one of Sheriff Graham's deputies, in dirty boots, a work shirt, and a vest. She smiled at me brightly from beneath a neat-looking cowboy hat which sat on top of her thick, blonde curls.

"I hate to see any kid go hungry," she told me, "even though you look like you've never missed a meal in your life."

She pointed at my stomach and laughed. I looked down at my belly and frowned.

Alright, I'm a little heavy. So what? It's not a crime. It's just that I really love food, and I really hate exercise. You would hate exercise too if you were as clumsy as I am. Every time I try to exercise, I end up stumbling into a snake's nest or tumbling down a rocky hill or falling into a well. I've fallen into so many wells that my father actually invented a specific type of machine to pull me out of them. He's gotten a lot of use out of that machine.

"That's not a very polite thing to say," I told her.

She scrunched up her face in confusion.

"Why not? It's true. You're chubby. I'm short. The man

sitting next to you is bald. That woman is wearing more makeup than a circus clown. And that guy over there has a ridiculous amount of hair growing out of his nose. There's nothing impolite about saying any of those things. It's just the truth."

"She's right!" said the man with the hairy nostrils as he burst into tears. "It's the awful truth!"

He ran out of the saloon with his hairy nose buried in his hands. Two of his friends ran after him, trying to console him about his nose hairs.

"I'm Iris," the girl told me, "but everyone calls me Shorty. What's your name, chubs?"

Chubs. What an awful nickname, I thought. *Then again, the kids at school call me Weirdo Waldo, so I suppose it could be worse.*

"My name is W.B.," I said to her. "It's nice to meet you, Shorty."

"What does W.B. stand for? Wide Butt?" Shorty asked and then giggled at her joke.

My face turned bright red. The mustachioed man walked up to me carrying my cheese sandwich. He didn't speak as he served me. He was still massaging the side of his glued mustache that Shorty had stretched. I stared at the sandwich, then at my belly, and no longer felt certain that I wanted to eat.

"It actually stands for Waldo Baron," I said quietly. "You know what? I think I lost my appetite. Thanks anyway, Shorty."

I hopped off my stool and started to walk out of the bar, wishing that I had never gone in there in the first place. But before I could cross the doorway, Shorty rushed over and stood in my way. She was so small that she barely came up to my belly button, but I could tell by the look on her little face that if I were to try to push her out of the way, I'd be in for quite a surprise. Some people just look tough, and she was one of those people. In her hand she held my cheese sandwich.

"I hurt your feelings?" she asked, looking confused.

I shrugged my shoulders.

"I'm sorry, W.B.," she said. "I didn't mean to. That's just the way everyone talks around here. Everyone makes fun of everyone. That's what we do with people we like. Take the sandwich. I'm sorry for hurting your feelings."

She held out the sandwich to me.

I still didn't appreciate being called Wide Butt, but I did appreciate that she was trying to be nice.

"Thanks," I told her as I accepted the sandwich, "but I should get going. I don't want to worry my parents. If they wake up and notice I'm gone they might be upset."

"Where're your folks?" Shorty asked.

"They're asleep in their flying house," I told her, and then I realized how odd that probably sounded.

Shorty raised one of her eyebrows.

"Excuse me?"

I explained to her that my parents were inventors who had turned our home into a giant flying machine, and that we were in Chicago to take part in the race around the country. Shorty seemed pretty impressed by that.

"That's amazing, W.B., a nationwide race! Wow. Why don't you look more excited about it? You have the same expression on your face that Pa does when Ma makes him clean a dead rat from the attic."

I was going to tell her about the Sheriff Graham show that I was missing back at home, but then I happened to glance outside and saw that Magnus was no longer at the hitching post.

"Where's my horse?"

Shorty turned and looked out the window.

"Was that your horse? The grey one with the funny looking saddle?" she asked.

"Yes."

"Oh, someone stole that horse. I watched it happen

while everyone in the saloon was laughing at you. Hey, want me to walk you home?"

Shorty and I split the cheese sandwich as we made the trip back to the Baron Estate. While we walked, Shorty told me about her parents, how they had recently moved to Chicago from Virginia, how she had a dream of one day owning a large ranch where she would train horses, how her mother was a great cook, how her father spent all of his time gluing animal tails to his face because he couldn't grow a real mustache, and how they all lived together in a little apartment over the saloon.

I tried to listen to her, but all I could think about was my parents and how furious they would be to learn that Magnus had been stolen. Magnus was an important part of the family. In fact, he was a more important part of the family than Aunt Dorcas. Magnus was much more useful around the house. And he rarely sang.

The walk was long, but since I had company, I didn't really mind. We reached the Exposition Fairgrounds after night had fallen. Most of the crowd had left. The inventors were all sleeping inside their inventions. The banana man was buried in his banana cart. Shorty walked me to the door of the Baron Estate and blushed when I invited her in for a cup of tea.

"Thanks, but no thanks," she said. "I have to get home. If I'm not there to help out with supper, Ma will get mad. But good luck with your race. It should be really exciting. I hope you have a great time."

She punched me on the shoulder, but it was a friendly sort of punch.

"Thanks," I said.

I tried to punch her back on the shoulder but missed, toppling over the front steps of the Baron Estate and landing headfirst in a hedge. After Shorty finished laughing—she laughed for a good fifteen minutes—she helped me out of the hedge and wished me goodnight.

"I'll come by tomorrow to see you off!" she called over her shoulder as she jogged down the street. "Goodnight, Wide Butt!"

I couldn't help but smile as I quietly opened the door. All of the lights were off, so I took a kerosene lantern from the table and lit it. I took a step forward and gasped.

There was a stranger seated on the sofa.

She was a beautiful woman with curly, black hair. On her head, she wore a dark cowboy hat with a red rose tucked into the band. She was dressed all in black, except for her boots, which were bright red. There was a big smile on her face.

"Hi there," she greeted me. "How're you doing?"

"Good," I said slowly. "And you?"

"Pretty well, thank you. Why don't you get comfortable? Take a load off. Have a seat, kid."

I walked over to my father's rocking chair across from the sofa, but I didn't sit down. The cheese sandwich that I had split with Shorty was suddenly churning in my stomach. Something was wrong. My parents wouldn't just invite some random stranger into our home. And speaking of my parents, where were they? I looked around the room and couldn't see M or P anywhere.

"Who are you?" I finally asked.

"My name is Rose," she said, "Rose Blackwood. I hope you don't mind, but I looked in your room and saw a bunch of those silly novels about that famous sheriff in Pitchfork, so I'm sure that you know all about my family. Let me tell you that I'm much prettier and nicer in real life."

The cheese sandwich that was churning in my belly started to bounce like dried corn in a hot skillet. I was more frightened than I'd ever been before. Suddenly I had one of those "out of body experiences" where my soul slipped out of my body and floated up to the ceiling. My soul noticed an open window and tried to make a break for it, but I caught it before it could get away. If I was going to be stuck in such a dangerous situation, then my cowardly soul was going to have to be stuck in it too.

Of course I had heard of her.

Rose Blackwood was Benedict Blackwood's little sister.

According to the Sheriff Graham stories that I had read, she was nearly as nasty as her older brother. I heard she once made a goldfish cry. By *yelling* at it.

Rose raised her right hand, which I could see was holding a little black pistol. I'd never had a pistol pointed at me before. Most people haven't, I suppose. Let me tell you, it's not particularly pleasant. In fact, it was so horrible that it made my upset stomach feel even worse.

Before I could stop myself, I belched.

And it was loud.

In fact, it was louder than I had ever belched before. It sounded like an angry troll trapped in a cave, and it lasted almost an entire minute. When I was finished, I blushed and excused myself. I could feel my face turning pink. Rose looked at me and frowned.

"Poor thing. Do you have a tummy ache?" she asked sympathetically.

I nodded my head.

"You should rest," she told me. "Why don't you sit down in that chair and get comfortable?"

She motioned for me to sit in the rocking chair. I tried to sit, but I was still so frightened that my legs didn't want to listen to me. I continued to stand there and stare at her. I couldn't believe that the sister of the most dangerous man in America was in my living room. If I wasn't so scared, I would have been excited. In fact, I might have even asked her for her autograph.

"Let me make this a little clearer for you, kid," Rose said after a moment. "Get comfortable or get shot."

The Vase That Was Stuck Over My Head Muffled My Words

I got comfortable. I got comfortable really fast.

Once I was seated, Rose told me what was going to happen.

"You're going to take me with you on this race," she said. "And I'm going to make sure you win."

"Thank you," I said.

"Don't interrupt me, kid. Once we've won, I'm going to take all of the prize money," she continued. "Then, you're going to fly this house to Pitchfork and help me break my brother out of jail. I figure I can use the prize money to hire some criminals to help us with that. I'm so glad that I read about the race in the newspaper. It's what gave me this great idea. You see, my folks have been bugging me to break Benedict out of jail for weeks. You should be proud to know that out of all the amazing vehicles in this race, this is the one that I thought had the best chance of winning."

The thought of breaking Benedict Blackwood out of jail was so terrifying and horrible that I immediately changed the subject. If I was forced to think about seeing that terrible man face-to-face, I might do something much worse than just burp.

"Where are my parents?" I asked in a shaky voice.

"They're tied up in their bedroom," Rose said as she walked over to the front door and locked it with a key that she must have taken from my parents. "Don't worry. They're both alright."

"What about Aunt Dorcas?" I asked.

Rose shuddered.

"I tied her up in her bedroom as well. She kept complaining about being kicked by a horse and bleeding on the inside. I hope you don't mind, but I tied a gag around her mouth to shut her up."

"That's fine," I told her, wondering

why we'd never thought to do that to Aunt Dorcas before. It seemed like such an obvious solution.

"So you understand my plan?" Rose asked. "I want to make sure that you do. The last thing I'd want would be for you to get hurt. I honestly care about your safety."

She said it in a kind tone that made me want to believe her, but it's very hard to believe that a person is kind when they're pointing a gun at you. I told this to Rose, but she disagreed.

"I'm pointing the gun at you *because* I care," she insisted. "It's to remind you not to try anything stupid, like attempting to trick me or trying to take my gun from me. Please don't even think about doing that, W.B. It would make me very sad if I had to hurt you. I'd cry about it for a week at least. Maybe even longer."

"I wouldn't be too happy about it either," I assured her. "Well, I understand your plan, and I won't do anything to stop you. Will you let me and my family go after your plan is done?"

"Of course," Rose said, sounding almost surprised by the question. "Why wouldn't I?"

"Ummmm," I hesitated before answering, "because you're an evil villain?"

Rose rolled her eyes as she took off her hat and placed

it on our coat rack.

"I've been very polite to you since we've met, haven't I?"

I find it best to agree with people who might shoot me, so I nodded my head. I nodded so hard that I almost fell out of my chair.

"Do you know that I've had this gun for five years?" she asked. "And I've never shot it before. Never. Not once. I hate the idea of having to use it. Do you know any evil people who hate using their gun?"

I shook my head so hard that I actually did fall out of my chair.

Rose frowned at me.

"Maybe I should stop asking you questions. You don't seem coordinated enough to answer. Why don't you go to bed, W.B.? I'm going to need you to be nice and well-rested for me tomorrow."

It seemed like a good idea. I picked myself up from the floor and ran up the stairs to my bedroom. Maybe I would wake up to find that this whole thing was nothing more than a terrible dream caused by a cheese sandwich.

I rested, but I didn't rest well. I had another talking

squirrel dream, but it wasn't the one I usually have. This time *I* was the one trapped in a cage. There was a giant squirrel which had Rose Blackwood's voice, and she was looking down at me. The giant squirrel laughed as she lifted my cage and threw it out of the flying Baron Estate. Before my cage crashed to the ground I awoke with a scream.

I opened my eyes.

Standing beside my bed was Rose Blackwood.

"Were you just screaming about squirrels?" she asked.

"No."

"Well, then get up and get dressed. I'll need you to be ready in about five minutes."

Rose started to walk out of my bedroom, but then she paused in the doorway.

"Don't wear anything as ugly as what you were wearing yesterday, though. There are going to be lots of people taking pictures of us. I don't want you to embarrass me."

But before I could ask her what was wrong with the clothes I had worn yesterday, she was already gone, closing the door quietly behind her.

I joined Rose in the living room, dressed in what I thought was one of my nicer outfits. She looked at me and frowned.

"That's still pretty awful," she said, as she spit in her palm and tried to fix my unfixable hair. "But I suppose it'll have to do. If any of these reporters ask who I am, I'm your sweet Auntie Rose. Got it? Tell them your parents are too busy steering the flying house to speak to them, so you and I will be the ones doing all the talking. Got it?"

I frowned as she fiddled with my hair, but of course I didn't complain. Rose was dressed in one of Aunt Dorcas's flowery dresses that buttoned high up on the neck, and she had slung one of her handbags over her shoulder. Her hair was put up in curls, and she wore a pair of Aunt Dorcas's round spectacles on her nose. She no longer looked like a dangerous bandit. She looked like someone's frumpy aunt, specifically *my* frumpy aunt. And my aunt is one of the frumpier aunts out there.

"How do I look?" she asked.

I was about to answer her honestly, but then I noticed that her handbag was slightly open. I could see her gun inside.

"You look like the prettiest woman in the world," I told Rose.

"Really? Aren't you sweet," she said with a smile as she patted her curls. "Are you ready?"

Before I could answer, Rose flung open the front door

to the Baron Estate. There was a shower of flashing lights, as there were dozens of people taking our picture with huge cameras set up on wooden legs. The crowd was even larger and louder than it was yesterday. Over a thousand people must have turned up to see all of the fantastic vehicles participating in the race.

A large stage had been set up across from the Baron Estate. There was a banner hanging from it that read "HORTENSE'S TOOTH POWDER! USE IT OR KISS YOUR TEETH GOODBYE!"

"How can a person kiss their own teeth?" I asked. Rose nudged me in the ribs.

Standing beneath the banner were three older men dressed in top hats and fancy suits. One of them held a cone shaped item in his hand, which Rose told me was a megaphone. He placed the smaller end of the megaphone to his lips and screamed out to the crowd:

"Ladies and gentlemen, boys and girls, fathers and mothers, daughters and sons, sisters and brothers, cousins and aunts and uncles, second cousins, great uncles, great aunts, cousins twice removed, foster parents, stepbrothers, stepsisters, half aunts, double uncles, and people who are of no relation to anyone . . . welcome to the first annual Hortense's Tooth Powder sponsored National Inventor's Race Around the Country!"

The crowd cheered. Several men threw their hats into the air. The ones without hats threw their wigs.

"We have invited inventors from all over the country, who have brought their fantastically unique vehicles; vehicles in which they will ride around this great nation in search of items from this list!"

He held up a piece of paper. Several flashbulbs went off as people tried to get a picture of the list.

List? I didn't remember M or P saying anything about a list.

"This list," the man continued, "contains ten items. They are completely random and unimportant household items, things like shoe polish, oatmeal, and dish soap. The people participating in this race will need to collect a *specific brand* of each item. Each of these brands can only be found in *one town* in the country, unlike Hortense's Tooth Powder, which is a brand that can be found nationwide. That's right, Hortense's Tooth Powder, *treat your tooth to a toothy treat!*"

"*Hor-tense!*" the other nicely-dressed men sang brightly as they waved their hands in a jazzy manner.

"Ahem. Anyway," the man said as he cleared his throat, "people participating in the race will need to travel to these ten towns and retrieve the ten items from the list, so we know for certain you've actually made your way around the country. It is proof that you aren't cheating. Once you've found all ten items, you will return here to Chicago. The first inventor to gather all ten items and return will be the winner and will be presented with five hundred dollars!"

The entire crowd went wild, cheering the idea of five hundred dollars.

"Isn't it remarkable?" Rose whispered to me. "Five hundred dollars! Isn't it exciting? Aren't you excited?"

She was smiling at me and squeezing my shoulder tightly, as though we were best friends.

"Seeing as how you're just going to steal the money from me and my family when we win," I told her, "no, not really. I can't say that I'm particularly excited."

Rose frowned at me.

"Well, maybe you can just be happy for me. If our positions were switched I'd be polite enough to be happy for you."

"Would you really?" I asked.

Rose thought about this for a moment.

"No," she admitted. "Probably not."

One of the men from Hortense's Tooth Powder came up to the Baron Estate to hand us the list of items we'd need to collect to prove we'd made it around the country.

"My goodness," he said as he looked in awe at the house. "This *is* fantastic. How did you get it to float here?"

"Not float, *fly*," I corrected.

"My apologies. How did you get it to fly here?"

"We have a thousand parakeets hidden in the basement," Rose told him with a smile as she reached for a copy of the list. "May I have our list, please?"

"Just a moment," the man said. "Before I can give you a copy of this, we need to have your entry fee, please."

Rose Blackwood frowned.

"Entry fee?" she asked. "What entry fee?"

"Five dollars and twenty-eight cents," the man told her, "Otherwise, you cannot take part in the race."

Rose turned to me with her mouth twitching. I could

see she was having trouble seeing out of Aunt Dorcas's glasses. She looked quite upset. I tried to smile widely at her to make her feel better, but she still frowned. I realized that I must have looked like a big blur to her because of the glasses, so I tried to smile even wider.

"My dear, young lad!" the well-dressed man scolded me. "Don't make that horrible face at your mother. You look like a nauseated fish."

"It's alright," said Rose. "And he's my nephew, not my son. I would never let my son walk around dressed in silly clothes like that. W.B., do you happen to have five dollars and twenty-eight cents you can lend to your pretty auntie?"

She flashed a sweet smile at me.

"No," I said. "But M and P do. I could go ask them for it."

I turned to find my parents, but before I could take a single step, Rose's hand gripped my wrist.

"That won't be necessary, dear," she said, giving my wrist a squeeze. "I will get it from them. Just stay here and don't do anything foolish, alright?"

Shaking the handbag with her gun in it at me, Rose stumbled blindly down the hall to find my parents, bumping into the table, then the doorway, and then walking face first into the wall.

I stood there in the doorway with the man from Hortense's Tooth Powder, who clearly had no idea what to say to me.

"So . . ." he said slowly, "do you like tooth powder?"

"Sure. It's okay."

Before he could think of another thing to ask me (presumably about tooth powder) a small kid shoved her way through the crowd and over to the Baron Estate. It was Shorty.

"Hey there, W.B." she said with a bright smile. "Today's the big day!"

While it was nice to see my new friend, I was still feeling pretty terrible about my current predicament. I wished that I could tell her what was happening with Rose Blackwood and my parents.

"Yup," I told her and tried to smile back.

My mouth was fighting me. It really didn't want to form a smile. So I had to force it, using all of the muscles in my cheeks as well as three of my fingers.

Shorty raised an eyebrow at me.

"What's wrong with your face?" she asked. "You look like a chipmunk with hay fever."

Apparently when I try to make myself smile I look like a sick animal.

"Nothing is wrong," I told her, glancing over my shoulder. "I'm just waiting for my Aunt Rose to come back with the entry fee for the race."

"Huh?" said Shorty, as she scratched her blonde curls. "Aunt Rose? I thought your aunt's name was Dorcas. I remember you telling me that because it's the silliest name I've ever heard."

I could feel a drip of sweat run down my forehead. The Hortense's Tooth Powder man was yawning and glancing at his pocket watch. I wanted very badly to tell Shorty that Rose wasn't my aunt, that she was a villain who was planning on robbing us and forcing us to help her free the evilest man in the country from jail. But I couldn't. If I said anything, who knows what Rose would do to M and P.

"It is," I finally said to Shorty, and then I squeezed my lips together with my fingers.

Shorty raised her other eyebrow at me.

"OK. Well, in case I never see you again, I wrote you a letter," she reached into her pocket and pulled out an envelope. "It has my address on it. Maybe when you get back to Pitchfork, you can write to me too."

She handed me the letter. It was a very sweet gesture.

More importantly, it gave me an idea.

"Let me give you my address right now," I told her.

"Although you might need to wait a while before mailing me anything because my house will be flying around the country, and I don't think the mailman will be able to catch it. Ummm, Hortense's Tooth Powder man? Do you have an extra piece of paper I could borrow?"

The man gave me a little sheet of paper and a pencil. I wrote down my address, and at the top of the paper I wrote: ROSE BLACKWOOD!!!

I folded the paper and handed it to Shorty, who smiled.

"Thanks!" she said, and then she quickly hopped into the air and gave me a kiss on the cheek before disappearing back into crowd.

It was the first kiss I'd ever been given by anyone other than my mother or Aunt Dorcas, and those kisses didn't really count. Especially not Aunt Dorcas's, which were always so wet and gross and slimy and eggy and—*oh my gosh she might* actually *be part egg.*

"That's very cute," Rose said as she came back to the doorway. "I didn't know you had a girlfriend, W.B. What's her name?"

It took me a moment to remember Shorty's real name.

"Iris," I told her. "Her name is Iris."

Rose smiled.

"There's nothing lovelier than a woman named after a

flower," she said, and then turned to the Hortense's Tooth Powder man and handed him the entry fee. "Here is our fee. May we have our copy of the list now, please?"

When the door was closed, Rose Blackwood took off Aunt Dorcas's glasses, unpinned her hair, and pulled her gun from the handbag.

"Ooh, my head," she said as she rubbed her eyes. "I understand why that woman is always complaining. If my eyes were that bad I'd probably go around wearing a pair of eye patches like my old Uncle Patches used to. Boy, I miss him. He died last year after accidentally riding a donkey backwards off a cliff. The poor guy never saw it coming."

She glanced at the clock on the mantle and then quickly sat on the sofa and gripped the armrest.

"W.B., you might want to sit down or grab a hold of something," she warned.

"Why?"

Suddenly the Baron Estate jerked to one side, and then to the other side. In an instant I was upside down at the other end of the room with a large vase stuck over my head.

"That's why," Rose said with a frown. "It's 12:01. The race has officially started. Our first stop is in Stone Lake, Massachusetts. According to this list, we will need to find bottle of Stone Lake Shoe Polish. Are you ready?"

I tried to tell her that I was, but the vase that was stuck over my head muffled my words.

THE EGG HAD
FLOWN THE COOP!

"**R**un!" Rose screamed.

I ran.

Two dozen wild pigs squealed in anger as they chased us. They were large and hairy with huge tusks sticking out of the corners of their mouths. I had a bottle of Ruttleshlub Hair Tonic shoved under my arm.

"Don't drop that bottle again!" Rose warned me. "If you do, we'll have to turn back and get another one. And you know how crazy it'll be in Ruttleshlub once the other inventors get there!"

"SQUEEEEAAAL!" the wild pigs squealed behind us.

"I thought pigs were supposed to be nice!" I gasped, feeling lightheaded.

I really hate running. I really, really hate it.

"Did you expect them to invite us over for tea or something?" Rose asked. "They're wild animals! This is what they do! Run faster, kiddo! They're gaining on you!"

I turned my head to look at the pigs and then immediately wished that I hadn't. She was right. The wild pigs were gaining on me, and they appeared to have doubled both in number and in size. They looked as large as rhinoceroses and twice as mean.

Rose continued to run as fast as she could. My brain ordered my legs to keep moving, but my legs had other ideas. In fact, my legs were suggesting that we stop for a moment to take a break, perhaps even a quick nap. My lungs were also in favor of stopping, and my heart and stomach and kidneys and spleen were leaning in that direction as well. In fact, my brain was the only part of my body with any interest in continuing to run, and it was quickly being overruled by the rest of me.

Did I mention that I hate running?

"Stop chasing me!" I called to the pigs. "Please stop chasing me? I promise never to eat bacon again if you stop chasing me! Or pork! Or ham! Or even sausage!"

The pigs didn't seem to care about my promises—which, I admit, were lies—and continued to run. It turns out that you can't bargain with wild pigs. This was turning out to be a very educational adventure.

Rose Blackwood reached the Baron Estate and threw open the front door.

"Hurry up!" she cried.

"I'm hurrying!" I gasped.

"Well, hurry faster!"

There are few things that are less helpful than someone telling you to "hurry faster." As if my legs and feet will suddenly say, "Oh, you mean hurry *faster*? I thought you wanted me to hurry *slower*. Silly me, I'm always getting those two confused."

The wild pigs were still gaining on me, and I could now smell them as well as hear them. They sounded angry, and somehow they smelled angry too, though I can't quite explain to you how an animal can smell angry. They just did.

The Baron Estate was just up ahead. It was so close. I only needed to sprint for another twenty seconds, and I was going to make it. *I'm going to be alright.* Soon I'd be locked in the safety of the house I'd lived in for all my life. My parents and I would be laughing about this later. I was sure of it. We would all be laughing about this silly little misadventure. In fact, I was so certain that everything would be alright that I started laughing.

"Haha! Hahahaha! Haaa—"

As I laughed, I slipped and fell face forward into the mud.

I suppose I should fill you in on what happened between the start of the race and the pig incident. The pig incident is where I'm lying face down in a mud puddle in Ruttleshlub, California, which, incidentally, is not a particularly pleasant incident. It was a very eventful couple of days. In fact, it would all have been quite exciting if I hadn't had a large amount of mud stuffed into my ears, and an even larger amount stuffed into my nostrils, and the dozen or so wild pigs who were about to stomp me into a lumpy custard.

Anyway, here is what happened after the Baron Estate left Chicago.

"It's amazing," Rose said to me as the Baron Estate continued to sail through the sky, gliding smoothly over the clouds like a square-shaped bird with no wings. "I didn't think that flying machines were possible, and I certainly never dreamed that a *house* could become a flying machine. Your parents must be two of the smartest people in the world."

"Umm," I said, rubbing my forehead, which was still a bit sore from the vase, "speaking of my parents . . . could I please see them? They must be worried about me. I promise not to do anything stupid. Or smart. Or both. Please. Just let me see them."

Rose frowned at me for a moment as she unbuttoned the high collar of Aunt Dorcas's dress.

"I suppose that's alright," she finally said. "I want to change out of this dreadful dress anyway. I'll allow you to visit your parents for five minutes, but no longer than that. And if you like, you can visit your aunt for five minutes as well."

"No, that's okay," I said, as I made my way out of the living room. "I wouldn't want to bother her."

Or have her bother me. Aunt Dorcas always made everything seem a thousand times worse than it actually was. And since we were being kidnapped by the sister of the world's most dangerous man, my aunt would be absolutely unbearable to listen to right now. Listening to her would be like stuffing an agitated chicken into my brain.

I opened the door to the garage. My father was seated at the wheel. Or to be more specific, his body was tied to the wheel, with each wrist and ankle tied around a different peg sticking out of the outer portion of the wheel. If he wanted to make a wide turn, he had to spin all the way around; this would cause him to flip upside down which, strangely enough, he seemed to enjoy.

My mother was tied to a table underneath the map of the world, beside the panel and lever which controlled the speed of the house. The end of her long pencil was stuck in her teeth. She was still using it to point out the route we should be taking to Massachusetts.

"No, you're putting us off course," she said to my father. "I said make a thirty-*five* degree turn. You made a thity-*seven* degree turn."

"That's easier said than done, my little muffin," my father replied as he continued to spin around and around on the wheel. "I appear to be going in circles right now, but when I've righted myself I will be certain to correct the angle of my turn. Wheeee!"

"I'm alright!" I called out. "It's okay! You can stop worrying about me now!"

For a moment neither of them spoke. They looked quite surprised to hear my voice. I wonder if they had trouble recognizing it.

"Oh," said M. "Good. I'm so glad to hear that, W.B."

"Yes," my father said unconvincingly, "I was very worried."

"Very worried," my mother echoed.

I frowned. They had both clearly forgotten about me and were completely focused on flying the Baron Estate.

"You weren't worried," I said darkly. "I can tell. What's wrong with you two? I've been stuck out there with a madwoman who has a gun!"

"She may have a gun, but at least she's polite," M said. "She made certain that we were quite comfortable when she tied us up. And she regularly comes in to shovel coal and to let us have breaks for tea and snacks and to use the bathroom. Oh, and she makes the most delicious split pea soup I've ever tasted. I must get the recipe from her before she leaves."

"Your mother is right," said P, as he finally stopped spinning. "As far as kidnappers go, Rose is one of the better ones. We should consider ourselves lucky."

"Very lucky," my mother echoed.

"Lucky?" I said, unable to believe what I was hearing. "No! Absolutely not! This is not lucky! *Lucky* is when you find a penny on the street, or when you drop a glass and it doesn't break, or when you're about to roll out of a floating house and you miss the open front door by a few inches."

"*Flying* house," P corrected, "not floating."

"Lucky is not getting kidnapped!" I snapped, as I looked at the cuckoo clock on the wall to check the time. "I can't believe how well you're taking all of this."

P and M tried to exchange a glance, but they couldn't because they were both tied up tightly. So instead they just rolled their heads around and pretended they were exchanging a glance before turning back to me.

"W.B.," my mother said gently, "what good would it do to get upset? The smartest thing we can do is to listen to Rose Blackwood and do what she says."

"And she says she'll let us go once she's freed her brother from jail," my father added as he adjusted the turn by leaning to the left.

"And you believe her?" I asked. "But she's a horrible, terrible, lying, stealing, thieving, no-good-dirty-rotten criminal!"

I then heard the sound of someone clearing their throat behind me.

Oh . . . fiddlesticks.

I held my breath and turned around. Rose Blackwood was standing there with a frown on her face.

"Didn't your parents ever teach you that it's rude to call people names?" she asked.

"That was mean, W.B. I think you need to apologize to her," said P.

"What?" I asked, my eyes growing wide with disbelief. "Seriously? Apologize to our kidnapper?"

"Yes. W.B., apologize to our kidnapper right this second!" my mother ordered.

I couldn't believe my ears. They really expected me to apologize to Benedict Blackwood's sister. I felt like I was living in a madhouse—in an upside down madhouse. Suddenly the cuckoo clock next to my head chimed. A tiny cuckoo bird popped out of a little door in the center of it and poked me in the eye.

"Ow!" I cried. "I'm sorry, okay?"

"Be careful, W.B." my father scolded. "That's the twelfth time you've been poked in the eye by that cuckoo bird. I bought that clock in Switzerland, and I really don't want you to break it."

"You must be the clumsiest kid in the world," said Rose as she shook her head.

"He really is," my mother agreed.

"It's true," P chuckled.

"W.B., why don't you go visit your Aunt Dorcas?" Rose suggested. "I need to talk with your parents for a moment."

"That's alright," I told her quickly, "I'll just go to my room and sit alone in the dark. I should be punished anyway."

"W.B., go visit your Aunt Dorcas!" M ordered. "That is your punishment!"

"Go right now!" my father said, and then he started to

spin again. "Wheeeeeeeeeeeee!"

I grumbled my way out of the garage, up the stairs, and then down the hall to Aunt Dorcas's room. I seemed to be doing a lot of grumbling lately. As I grumbled, I rubbed my sore eye. I really hated that stupid cuckoo clock. Maybe my parents and Rose Blackwood were right. Sometimes it did seem like I was the clumsiest kid in the world.

I reached my Aunt Dorcas's room and knocked on the door. I hoped that she would tell me to go away, and that she wasn't interested in having any visitors. The last thing I wanted was to listen to her clucks and cries and complaints.

But there was no answer.

I knocked again. And again. And then one more time just to be sure she'd heard me.

"Aunt Dorcas?" I called. "It's me. W.B. Are you okay?"

There wasn't a sound.

I twisted the doorknob and discovered that it was unlocked.

Of course it was unlocked, I told myself. She's tied up in bed. Rose Blackwood told me so. I pushed the door open, and, to my surprise, the room appeared to be completely empty.

"Aunt Dorcas?" I said, looking around. "Aunt Dorcas?"

I checked underneath the bed and in her closet. I looked behind the door and behind the large dresser. Then I went to the window and looked outside. We were still flying high above the clouds and moving at a steady rate.

Aunt Dorcas was gone.

The egg had flown the coop!

WHY DOES IT SMELL LIKE FEET IN HERE?

We reached Stone Lake, Massachusetts an hour later, landing in a large and empty valley surrounded by nothing but flat rocks.

"Where are all the lakes?" Rose Blackwood asked as she looked out the window. "I was hoping to change into my bathing suit and go for a swim."

"I suppose the lakes are all made of stone," I said, pointing to the rocks. "I wouldn't recommend diving into them if I were you."

She made a face at me and tweaked my nose.

"Don't be such a smart mouth, W.B., or I'll force you to stay in Aunt Dorcas's room."

It suddenly struck me that I was the only one in the

Baron Estate who realized that Aunt Dorcas had somehow escaped her room and was currently missing. Where was she? I began to back out of the living room towards the hallway where I could start a real search for her. The Baron Estate was pretty large, and there were lots of little nooks and crannies where a crafty egg like her could hide.

As I was slowly backing out of the room, Rose reached out and caught me by the hand.

"Where do you think you're slowly backing off to?" she asked. "You're coming with me to find the Stone Lake Shoe Polish from the list."

"Oh. Errr, right."

After I had put on my coat and my hat and Rose Blackwood had changed back into Aunt Dorcas's frilly clothes, we were out the door and crossing the stony plain. We could see a small town just up ahead, and a large wooden sign that told us where we were and how many people lived there. The sign read:

WELCOME TO
STONE LAKE, MASSACHUSETTS.
POPULATION: WE ACTUALLY
HAVEN'T GOTTEN AROUND TO
COUNTING EVERYBODY YET. BUT WE

WILL. IT'S JUST BEEN A REALLY BUSY
WEEK. WE SHOULD BE FINISHED
COUNTING EVERYONE BY
TOMORROW.

The sign looked very old.

As we walked into town, Rose took me firmly by the hand.

"I can walk by myself," I told her.

"First of all, no you can't," she told me. "You fall down and hurt yourself so often that I sometimes wonder how you're still alive. Secondly, I'm holding on to you to make sure you don't run off and try to get back to the Baron Estate without me. I don't trust you."

"*You* don't trust *me?*" I said with a frown. "But you're an evil villain. I'm just a kid."

"You're a mean kid," Rose replied. "I've never said anything bad about you, but you told your parents all sorts of terrible things about me. How do you think that makes me feel?"

I looked at Rose as though she were crazy. In fact, she must have been a little bit crazy to believe that. I'd never heard of an evil villain who gets upset when you call them an evil villain.

"You and your family are criminals," I said to her, lowering my voice when we passed by the other people in town. "You do terrible things. That makes you a terrible person. I'm only telling the truth."

Suddenly I thought of Shorty and what she had said to me after she hurt my feelings by calling me Wide B—I mean, by calling me that mean name that I don't remember.

Rose frowned at me and started to respond, but then she spotted Stone Lake General Store on the corner of the road.

"You don't know as much as you think you do, Waldo Baron," Rose whispered as she led me into the store.

"Good morning, strangers," the man behind the counter at the general store said as he thumbed through a newspaper on the counter.

"Good morning," said Rose.

"Good morning," I said, looking around. "What sort of stuff do you sell here?"

"General stuff," the man replied as he licked his thumb and turned a page in his newspaper.

"Over here!" Rose hissed and dragged me to the part of the store where the shoe polish was.

Blue Shack's Shoe Black. Shoshanna's Shoe Shine. Polish Polly's Polish. Snoodle Magloo's Shoe Goo. There were several different brands of shoe polish on the shelf, but not one of them was Stone Lake Shoe Polish.

"Excuse me, sir?" Rose called to the man behind the counter. "You don't happen to carry Stone Lake Shoe Polish, do you?"

"Yes I do, ma'am," the man responded, as he licked his index finger and turned another page in his paper.

"Oh really? Have you run out of it then?" I asked.

"No, sir, I did not," the man said, licking his middle finger and turning another page.

"Do you have some more of it in the back room?" Rose asked hopefully.

"Yes ma'am, I do," the man said, licking his little finger and turning *yet another* page.

"Do you really need to lick a different finger each time you turn a page?" I asked.

He licked one of the fingers on his other hand (one of the fingers that he wasn't using to turn pages in his newspaper) and then turned another page.

"Yes, sir. Yes, I do."

"We'll take one bottle of Stone Lake Shoe Polish, please," said Rose, offering a little curtsy and forcing me to do the same.

The man behind the counter licked his ring finger and set the newspaper onto the counter. He disappeared into the back room of the store. After a moment, he returned with a single bottle of Stone Lake Shoe Polish. Rose smiled as she dragged me to the register.

"You have money, right?" she whispered to me.

I thought of the handful of coins I had in my pocket and nodded. I didn't have much, but I certainly had enough for shoe polish. And who knows? If Rose Blackwood was really as nice and fair as my parents seemed to think she was, maybe she'd even pay me back.

"Alright," said the man behind the counter. "That'll be fifty dollars and twenty-two cents."

Rose's jaw dropped so far and so fast that it unbuttoned the top button of Aunt Dorcas's high-necked dress.

"Fifty dollars?" she breathed.

"And twenty-two cents," the man added. "Ma'am, your collar came undone. If you need a button to fix that, we have them available for one cent."

"Why are buttons only one cent but shoe polish is fifty dollars?" I asked.

"And twenty-two cents," the man added, sounding a bit annoyed. "Don't think you'll get out of paying that twenty-two cents."

"Why on earth would you charge so much for shoe polish?" Rose asked.

The man behind the counter adjusted his hat and

glasses and then licked both of his index fingers before holding up his newspaper for us to see. On the front page of the paper was an article about our race.

"Hortense's Tooth Powder sent us a telegram last week requesting that we make sure to have plenty of Stone Lake Shoe Polish in stock," the man told us with a syrupy grin. "They explained that you inventors will need to pick up a bottle of it in order to complete your wacky race around the country. This is the only store in town that sells it, so if you want to finish your race and win five hundred dollars, then it's going to cost you a pretty penny. Actually, it'll cost you 5,022 pretty pennies, to be specific, though I'll accept ugly pennies too."

I could see Rose Blackwood begin to tremble with rage. Her eyes were burning holes into the smug face of the general store owner. I started to feel a bit nervous. After all, she was Benedict Blackwood's sister. And I had heard that Benedict Blackwood once shot a cloud to stop a rainstorm that was bothering him . . . and it actually worked.

"Do you think the owners of Stone Lake Shoe Polish would appreciate you raising the price of their product without asking them?" she asked quietly.

The man laughed as he licked his knuckles.

"Lady, it was their idea!" he chortled.

"You seriously need to stop licking your hands," I told him. "It's disgusting. You handle money and other items all day. You're going to get sick."

Suddenly we heard a thundering stampede from outside. I looked out the window and saw the large group of inventors chugging down the street as quickly as they could. They were still dressed in their white inventor coats and goggles, their hair flying wildly in the breeze. I recognized all of them: the men with the flying train car, the women with the land ship, the boys with the giant rocket, the family with the electric powered fish-thing, and even the man with the banana cart.

Wait, how did the banana man get here so quickly?

When the other inventors spotted the general store they made a mad dash for it, knocking over fruit carts, scaring horses, toppling towering displays of canned goods, crashing into a couple of men who were carrying a large mirror, and stopping only to allow a duck and her thirty-seven ducklings to the cross the street.

"Come on!" one of the inventors yelled at the ducklings. "Cross faster!"

When the ducklings had finished crossing the street, the inventors swarmed the general store.

"Alright!" the owner called happily, licking both of his thumbs. "Come right in! I have exactly what you need. If you'll just line up in an orderly fashion, I will collect fifty dollars and twenty-two—"

But the inventors weren't interested in lining up in an orderly fashion. They were interested in tearing through the store and knocking everything off the shelves as they searched for the shoe polish.

"Now see here!" the owner cried, licking his pinky fingers. "Stop this madness!"

But the inventors weren't interested in *seeing here* or *stopping this madness*. They continued to rip the shelves apart, moving like hungry dogs as they searched every corner of the store for the shoe polish.

"Please!" the owner bellowed, licking his nose as he began to panic. "Please stop destroying my store!"

He rushed into the backroom and came back out with a box full of Stone Lake Shoe Polish.

"Here!" he screamed. "Here, you mad fools! Take it! Each bottle is fifty dollars and twenty-two ce—"

The swarm of inventors swallowed him up, ripping the box from his hands as they each tried to grab a bottle of shoe polish.

Rose and I stood there in wide-eyed shock as we watched the inventors act like piranha fish.

"They look like monsters," Rose whispered to me.

"I don't think so," I said. "I'll bet monsters are usually better behaved than this."

Rose nodded in agreement.

The inventors then began to fight one other for the shoe polish, pulling each other's hair, tearing one another's white coats, and tugging on the goggles which they wore fastened around their heads with rubber bands and then letting go, which caused them to snap back into their faces.

"Ouch!" cried an inventor whose face had just been thwacked by his own goggles. "That really hurts!"

In the tussle, a bottle of Stone Lake Shoe Polish was accidentally thrown into the air. Rose and I watched the bottle spin, almost in slow motion, as it flew all the way across the store . . . and bonked me on the head. Rose picked up the bottle and stuck it in her bag.

"Ow."

Rose shook her head at me.

"Maybe you're cursed," she said, patting me gently on the shoulder. "Well, we have the shoe polish. Now it's time to go."

I took a step towards the door, but Rose caught me by the collar of my coat.

"Wait," she said. "How much do the other brands of shoe polish cost?"

I took a look at the shoe polish tins and bottles which were scattered all over the floor. The inventors continued to quarrel and fight with one another while using the general store owner's back as their battleground. I could hear him trying to scream for help, but unfortunately his mouth was muffled by his own knee.

"It looks like most of these just cost a few pennies," I told Rose.

"Alright," she said, "then leave a few cents on the counter."

I did as I was told, taking three of my coins and leaving them next to the cash register on the counter.

"Thank you!" the owner said to us from underneath several dozen stomping feet. "Have a nice day!"

Rose Blackwood and I both had huge smiles on our faces as we returned to the Baron Estate. I know I shouldn't have been smiling since I was still being kidnapped, my parents were still tied up in the control room, and Aunt Dorcas was wherever Aunt Dorcas was, but it was actually pretty exciting now that the race had started.

"Why did you make me pay for the shoe polish?" I asked Rose. "We could have just taken it."

"That would be stealing," Rose told me. "While it was wrong for that man to raise the price of the shoe polish to take advantage of the people trying to win the race, it was even more wrong of the inventors to ruin his store and try to steal from him."

Once again I felt as though the world had gone mad. I was getting lectured by a criminal about stealing. That was like getting lectured by a fish for drinking too much water, or by a bear for going to the bathroom in the woods.

"But . . ." I began, "but you're *Rose Blackwood.*"

"Yes. And you're *Waldo Baron.* Now let's go tell your parents that it's time to move on to the next town on our list. This is rather fun, isn't it?"

She threw open the door to the work garage and immediately made a sour face.

"Why does it smell like feet in here?"

I Felt Like a Marshmallow Wrapped in a Doily

"Hello you two!" my father called happily, wiggling his bare toes. "How's the weather in Stone Lake?"

I had to place my hand over my nose as well. It did stink like feet in the garage. I looked over at M and saw that her feet were now bare as well.

"Rose, my dear," M said with a concerned look on her face. "There's something that McLaron and I forgot to mention to you. We were supposed to pick up more coal in Chicago, but we forgot. And now we have almost no coal left. This is our fault, and we apologize to you for the inconvenience."

"We need to keep the furnace going," P pointed to the furnace with his big toe. "It needs to burn because it is powering the flying Baron Estate. Since our hands are tied, we slipped off our boots and kicked them into the furnace, along with our socks. Sorry for the stink. That must be the smell of our burning socks. Perhaps we should wash our socks more often, eh Sharon?"

"You're welcome to wash our socks anytime you like, McLaron," M told him.

They started to bicker about whose job it was to wash their socks, and as they argued I found myself growing more and more frustrated with them.

"Stop arguing!" I finally said.

To my surprise, they actually stopped.

"W.B. is right," M said. "It's rude to argue in front of our guest. I'm sorry, Rose."

"Yes," agreed my father with an apologetic bow of his head. "That is very rude of us. I apologize, Rose."

As he bowed his head the wheel began to spin.

"Wheeeeeeeeeeeeee!"

"Why do you keep apologizing to her?" I asked. "You didn't get more coal in Chicago because she tied you up and threatened you. It's her fault that you ran out of coal."

"W.B.," M said sternly.

"Wheeeeeeeeeeeeeeeeee!"

"No, he's right," Rose said. "It is my fault. And I apologize, Mr. and Mrs. Baron. So what can we do? I didn't see any coal in the general store. Do we have enough to get us to Bortstown, New Jersey? That's where the next item is."

"Nope," said P after he'd finished spinning. "We only have enough to go another two hundred and fifteen yards. We need to start burning something else, and we need to start burning it fast. Is there anything outside that we can burn to power the Baron Estate? Any trees?"

Rose shook her head. "Nope. Stone Lake is completely covered in stone. I don't suppose you can burn stone, can you?"

"No," M said with a frown, "I suppose we can burn some furniture and other household items that we don't really need."

"Like the cuckoo clock?" I asked hopefully.

"I was thinking more like books," M said. "W.B., you have the largest book collection in the house. Please go fetch some of them and bring them in here. We'll burn them, along with the two chairs from the living room, the desk from our bedroom, and your father's collection of unusual hats."

"Awww, not my unusual hats," my father lamented. "I love those."

"You never wear them," my mother argued.

"Well you love your antique flowerpots, but you never wear those either."

"Please don't make me burn my books," I begged. "Let me burn my clothes instead."

"That's not such a bad idea," Rose commented. "The boy's clothes are so ugly that sometimes I get a stomach-ache from looking at him."

"Yes, but he needs his clothes," M told her. "He might get strange looks from people if he goes around without them. I suppose we can burn Aunt Dorcas's luggage, doll collection, and the little wooden boxes she keeps on her dresser."

"Alright, I'll get them for you," Rose said.

My heart skipped. If Rose learned that Aunt Dorcas had escaped, she might get so angry that she'd forget how much she hates using her gun. I couldn't risk it. I would have to keep her from going in there and discovering the truth.

"No, that's alright," I said quickly. "I'll go get everything. I could use the exercise. And I do owe you an apology, Rose. I'm sorry. So sorry. Can I get anyone anything to eat while I fetch those things? I'm going to make Aunt Dorcas a sandwich and maybe a hardboiled egg. She must be hungry. I know that I am. And then she'll probably want to go right to sleep after she eats. And of course, you should never wake a sleeping Dorcas. Right? Right."

Before anyone could respond, I zipped out of the garage, zipped down the hall, zipped up the stairs, and zipped back to Aunt Dorcas's door. I walked inside (I was tired of zipping) and saw that the room was still empty. My aunt hadn't returned. So I went to the closet and pulled out her extra pillows and stuffed them underneath the blanket on her bed so it would look as though she was under there.

After I collected her little wooden boxes, suitcases, and some of her uglier dolls, I ran back to the garage.

Rose was breaking up our living room chairs and throwing them into the furnace on top of the coal. As everything caught fire and began to burn, my mother turned a knob on the control panel and I felt the house begin to move.

"Toss that stuff into the furnace and then help me smash this furniture," Rose said, handing me a hammer. "Your father said if we throw all of this furniture and your aunt's useless junk into the furnace, we'll be able to reach New Jersey in an hour or two."

We smashed and broke up all of the extra furniture that we could, tossing it into the angry sounding furnace as the Baron Estate continued to move, flying swiftly into the bright and sunny afternoon.

Bortstown, New Jersey was exactly like Stone Lake, Massachusetts, except that it wasn't.

I mean, it didn't look like Stone Lake at all. It was a larger city with paved streets, and the sign that stated it was Bortstown actually listed how many people lived there. Sort of.

WELCOME TO
BORTSTOWN, NEW JERSEY.
POPULATION: 11,111 . . . GIVE OR TAKE.

But shortly after we got there and found the store that sold the item we were supposed to collect (Bortstown Oatmeal), the other inventors showed up and absolutely destroyed the little store. I mean it was really bad this time. The shelves were shattered, the walls were cracked, several of the floorboards were ripped up, and someone accidentally set the owner's grandmother on fire.

Rose and I were forced to go to another store to buy a wheelbarrow and a huge pile of coal so that we could continue our trip without burning any more furniture or stinky socks. We took turns pushing the large wheelbarrow across town, back to where my parents had parked the Baron Estate.

"I still can't believe how poorly these inventors are behaving. They're acting like criminals," Rose said as she shook her head in disappointment. "I bet they'll never host another contest like this one ever again. It's a shame to see how terribly people will act just to win some money."

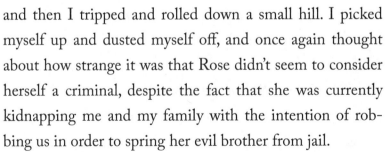

I rolled my eyes as I rolled the wheelbarrow, and then I tripped and rolled down a small hill. I picked myself up and dusted myself off, and once again thought about how strange it was that Rose didn't seem to consider herself a criminal, despite the fact that she was currently kidnapping me and my family with the intention of robbing us in order to spring her evil brother from jail.

But as strange as I found her complaint, I had decided not to say anything about it. One reason why was because I'd already made a few comments to Rose about her being an evil criminal, and it didn't seem smart to test her temper.

The other reason why I didn't say anything was that I had noticed something strange as I struggled to push the wheelbarrow across town. And that "something strange" was currently occupying my normally unoccupied mind.

Someone was following us.

I first noticed the woman back in Stone Lake. She was pretty hard to miss. She was a tall woman with an exceptionally sharp and pointy looking nose. It was so sharp and pointy looking that I bet she could use it to peel carrots, though it would be rather odd if she did. She was dressed in blue with a small hat tied to her curly, brown hair, and she rode around on a bicycle with a basket tied to the front.

Unless this woman had a pointy-nosed twin who also lived in New Jersey, it meant that she was somehow following us. I'm not sure how she was doing it. Her bicycle was nice, but it certainly wasn't possible for it to follow a flying house all the way across two states in such a short amount of time. She might have been one of the other inventors, though I didn't recognize her from Chicago, and she certainly didn't seem interested in acquiring the items we needed to win the race, like the shoe polish and the oatmeal.

The pointy nosed woman followed us all the way to the Baron Estate, but when Rose and I approached the front door and looked over my shoulder, she seemed to have disappeared.

It was the strangest thing.

Well, not the strangest thing. The strangest thing would be if I woke up one morning to find that my night shirt had been stuffed with fish, my socks filled with custard, and my parents had somehow landed the Baron Estate on the dark side of the moon.

But this was still pretty strange.

"Scuttlebrick, North Carolina," Rose read from the list. "That's our next stop. We're making pretty good time, aren't we?"

"I suppose we are," said my father as he steered the house to the left. "W.B., would you mind resetting the clocks?"

"Why?" I asked. "What's wrong with them?"

"They're still set to Pitchfork time," M explained. "Since we're on the East Coast, we're now two hours ahead."

Rose and I frowned as we exchanged a confused look. We didn't understand what they were talking about.

"Two hours ahead of what?" I asked.

"Of Pitchfork," P answered.

"You mean we time traveled into the future?" Rose asked.

"We've traveled to a different time zone," P corrected.

"I suppose you can say we traveled through time," M said. "It has to do with our movement compared to the rotation of the earth. As the planet revolves around the sun, it continues to spin, which means it gets dark earlier in the East Coast than it does in the West Coast. So it's later here than it is back where we came from."

"Really?" Rose asked, her eyes growing as wide as dinner plates. "Does it work the other way around as well? I mean, if we moved really fast in the other direction, would we travel *back* in time?"

"Well, sort of, yes," my mother said. "If we were traveling in the other direction we would be crossing back into an earlier time zone."

"Then let's go!" Rose cried. "We'll travel back in time to the beginning of the race in Chicago, and we'll give ourselves the shoe polish and the oatmeal and the coal so we'll have a head start on everyone else!"

"I don't think you understand—" my mother began.

"Wouldn't that be cheating?" I pointed out to Rose.

"Plus, it would be dangerous to travel backwards in time. What if we crashed into ourselves?"

"What do you mean?" Rose asked. "You think we might crash into ourselves back in Chicago?"

"Not exactly," I told her. "I mean we might crash into ourselves somewhere between here and Chicago. You see, if we're traveling into the past, we'll have to pass by multiple earlier versions of ourselves in order to get to our earlier selves from Chicago."

"That's not how time zones work . . ." my father began.

"Son, you don't know what you're talking about," M said.

Though my parents kept telling me that I was getting it wrong, it all made perfect sense to me.

If there were earlier versions of ourselves in Chicago, it meant there were earlier versions of ourselves flying over every town and state we've traveled across since then. In fact, it meant that there was an earlier version of W.B. who just had that thought. And that thought. And that thought. And . . . I better stop now. I'm losing track of all of the W.B.s that exist. I had no idea there were so many W.B.s in the world. I wonder if they're all so clumsy.

"We might bump into any one of a million earlier versions of ourselves," I explained to Rose. "We might bump into them flying over Indiana, Ohio, or New York. They're all on the same path that we are, but they're living in different time zones. That's what my parents are saying."

"No, it really isn't," M said.

"Wait a minute," said Rose, as she rushed to the large picture window at the front of the garage. "Are we in danger of bumping into future versions of ourselves who are traveling back in time? Should we be on the lookout for them?"

She took out her gun.

"Oh dear," said M.

"Wheeeeeeeeeeeeeee!" said P as he began to spin.

"CUCKOOO!" cried the cuckoo as it popped out of the clock and stabbed me in the other eye.

"OW!"

While we had been making excellent time, we were hit with a delay just as the Baron Estate was hovering somewhere over North Carolina. Rose hadn't tied my father to the steering wheel properly after allowing him to use the bathroom, and part of his body came loose as the wheel began to spin from the force of the winds. P's head slapped against the floor so many times that we were certain he'd been knocked unconscious. But it turned out that he was fine. Apparently, in addition to giving him the world's strangest hair style, all of the lightning strikes had toughened up his skull.

As Rose and I tied him back to the wheel, we heard a *thump* and a *splat*.

"What was that?" Rose asked.

I looked up at the far right corner of the picture window. There was something stuck to it, something yellow and white and mushy. I pointed it out to Rose, and she made a face.

"Oh no," she groaned. "Did we just hit a bird or a giant bug?"

"I don't think so."

"Then what is it?" Rose asked.

"It looks like a banana."

"That's nonsense, W.B.," Rose scoffed. "What would a banana be doing up here in the sky?"

"Maybe a large bird was carrying it?"

"Why would a bird throw a banana at us?"

"Maybe it thought we were hungry?"

Before anyone could respond to that, the picture window was suddenly hit by five more bananas, as well as an orange, an apple, several strawberries, blueberries, rasp-berries, and a squishy old pear. Following the fruit salad attack, a series of inedible things began to beat against the Baron Estate as well: rocks, pebbles, sticks, empty bottles, and chunks of coal. We could hear it clattering against our other walls and our roof, hitting us from every imaginable direction. The sound echoed throughout the house like hail on a tin roof.

"We're under attack!" P declared. "Those bananas are a classic sign of gorilla warfare!"

We once again looked out the picture window of the work garage and realized that we were surrounded by unfriendly flying machines. And then we understood what was happening. The other inventors had apparently joined together to take out the competitor who they believed to be the biggest threat to win the race: us. They were going to stop us, one way or another, even if it meant knocking us out of the sky like we were an empty can sitting on a fencepost.

We watched as the inventors of the winged train car slid open their windows and hurled their lunches at us, perfectly good ham sandwiches, potato salad, and soft boiled eggs splattering on top of our roof. The men in the little, pedal-powered helicopter device began to throw marbles at our picture window, trying their best to shatter it. A pair of old ladies in a winged canoe flew over and began to bat at the Baron Estate with their paddles.

Those attacks were merely annoying (as well as a terrible waste of good food), but then we heard something that made us all gasp so hard that I'm pretty sure we sprained our vocal cords.

It was the terrifying *BOOM* of a cannon being fired.

We looked out of the eastern window of the work garage and saw one of the largest flying machines in the race: a pirate ship attached to a hot air balloon. It appeared to be an authentic pirate ship, complete with functional cannons poking out from the sides. We could see the inventors on that ship loading and lighting their cannons and aiming them straight at us.

I screamed. Rose screamed. M, who couldn't see what was happening because she was tied to the table, screamed as well. Only my father remained calm.

"P! You have to land the Baron Estate!" I cried. "They're going to blow us out of the sky!"

"Hmmmm," P hummed to himself, which he often does when he's just had an amusing thought.

"What is it?" I said.

"I've just had an amusing thought."

We all paused for a moment to hear what his amusing thought was, with the marbles and fruit and rocks and garbage and canoe paddles still tattooing the outside of the Baron Estate.

BOOM!

The pirate ship's cannons exploded again, and three cannonballs whizzed right by us, missing the Baron Estate only by a few feet. One of the cannonballs hit a small flying machine directly behind us, creating a large hole right in the center of its wing. A few seconds later, the small flying machine dropped from the sky like an exhausted seagull.

"McLaron?" M said through gritted teeth.

"Yes, my little muffin?"

"What's your amusing thought?"

P laughed to himself.

"Oh, I was just thinking about how predictable these inventors are. I knew they might try something like this, so when I was working on the flying Baron Estate's design, I included a series of weapons which would protect the entire house from an aerial attack. I built little hidden cannons all along the base of our home. Do you see that red button on the wall? If you press it, all of those little cannons will fire at once."

"They will?" Rose asked. "So we're saved! That's fantastic, Mr. Baron! W.B., go press the button!"

"Well . . . it *would* be fantastic," P continued, "but I never loaded the cannons with ammunition. I was going to put some rocks or pellets in them, but then I forgot."

All of our hearts sank. One of the pirate ship cannons fired yet again, and this time we heard a crunching sound from overhead. The entire Baron Estate shook.

"I think it clipped the chimney," M said in a worried tone. "McLaron, are you seriously telling me that we can't fight back? There's nothing in our cannons?"

"Well, not *nothing*," my father admitted, his face turning a bit pink from embarrassment (and also because the wheel had spun around halfway and he was turned upside down). "Remember how you're always telling me to clean up after Magnus when he makes his . . . ahem, *messes* right outside the kitchen window? Well, I didn't want to have to scoop up all of that waste and carry it over to the barn, so I just quickly shoveled it into the cannon chambers instead."

"You filled our cannons with horse plop?" I asked.

"I'm afraid so," said P. "I guess I got a bit lazy. If we survive this attack, I'll be sure to clean them out the next chance I get."

I looked at M. M looked up at Rose. Rose looked at me and nodded her head.

Before the flying pirate ship could fire another cannon-ball, I rushed to the red button on the wall and pushed it.

I won't go into detail about what happened next. Let's just say that the other inventors stopped bothering us after that.

Never underestimate the power of flying horse plop.

As the other inventors were forced to clean the disgusting mess from their vehicles, we arrived at our stop and picked up our next item from a Scuttlebrick, North Carolina general store.

The pointy nosed lady was in Scuttlebrick as well. She

followed Rose and me through town on her bicycle. I pretended not to see her. She also pretended not to see me. At one point we were too busy pretending not to see each other that we both walked face forward into a wall. I pretended that it didn't happen. She pretended that it didn't happen, too.

Soon we were back in the house. Night had fallen. As the Baron Estate continued to sail through the sky in search of our next stop, I sat at the window seat in the living room and stared into the darkness. I thought that the stars would be much easier to see with us being way up in the sky, but they still looked blurry and a million miles away.

Actually, they probably looked even blurrier to me because both of my eyes were still swollen from the stupid cuckoo clock and from walking face first into the wall. And at dinner time, I accidentally poked myself in the eye with my fork when I slipped on some creamed corn. It had not been a very good day for my eyes.

"There sure are a lot of them, aren't there?" a voice from behind me said. "Stars, I mean."

Rose Blackwood sat next to me on the window seat. She had changed into a pair of M's pajamas.

"Yes," I agreed. "But if you want to know exactly how

many there are, you should ask my parents. I don't really know much about science."

"I sort of picked up on that," she said with a smile. "Don't worry. I don't either. My brother was always the smart one in our family. He actually did really well in school until he tied up the teacher and stole all of the desks from the schoolhouse. He also kidnapped the school gerbil, but his teacher commended his handwriting and grammar on the ransom note he left."

I shivered as I thought about her brother, Benedict Blackwood, who was said to be so mean and nasty that if you made him mad in a dream, he'd knock your lights out when he woke up.

"You don't seem to be anything like him," I told her.

"What do you mean by that?" she asked with a frown. "You're saying I'm not smart?"

"No. I mean, he has a reputation for being a cruel man who loves to lie and cheat and hurt people. And you . . . you're . . ."

"I'm what?" she asked.

I sighed. "Well, as much as I hate to say it . . . you're kinda nice. I mean, other than the part about you kidnapping my family, threatening to rob us, and forcing us to help you break your brother out of jail. If you ignore all of that stuff, you're actually a really nice lady."

I flinched again and covered my face in case she decided to prove me wrong by biffing me on the nose. But when I lowered my hands I saw that Rose wasn't angry. In fact, she looked really sad. She stared out the window into the darkness, and, for a moment, she didn't speak. And then I saw a single tear fall from her eye.

"Oh no," I said, suddenly feeling awful. "I didn't mean to make you cry. I take back what I said. You're just like your brother. You're an awful person and an evil villain, the absolute worst. I'm just an idiot with two black eyes who has strange dreams about squirrels. Don't listen to a thing I say."

"No, you're right," she said as she wiped her nose. "It's true. I mean, your thing about squirrels is really weird, but you're also right about me. I'm not a villain. I've never robbed or hurt anyone in my life. I'm just a failure who doesn't belong in her own family. My parents and my brother are famous villains with their pictures on wanted posters all across the country. And I've never even been late returning a library book."

I heard a creaking noise overhead, which sounded almost like a person slowly walking down the upstairs hall-ways. My mind immediately went to Aunt Dorcas. Was she out and about, prowling the house late at night? Was she even still in the house, or had she left while we were in Chicago or Massachusetts? Where in the world was that silly egg?

"I know the feeling, Rose," I told her as I stood up. "You've seen my parents, how brilliant they are and how much they love science. I'm nothing like them. I don't fit in with them either."

"Yes, but they love you, W.B.," she said. "Mine hate me. They really, really hate me."

"I'm sure that's not true," I said. "Say, I'm getting pretty sleepy. Goodnight."

"No, it's true," Rose insisted. "My parents tell me so all the time. 'We hate you, Rose. We really, really hate you.'"

"I'm sure they don't mean it."

"No, they do. They say 'We really, really mean it. We are not exaggerating. We really don't like you, Rose. For real.'" She buried her face in her hands and began to cry.

I felt terrible. I'd never seen anyone look so upset before. She was right about my parents. Even though I didn't understand them and I had nothing in common with them, I knew that they loved me and cared about me.

I went over to Rose and put my arm over her shoulder in a sort of half hug. At first she flinched when she felt my arm, but, when she realized that I was actually trying to be nice, she buried her head in my shoulder and hugged me back.

As I hugged Rose Blackwood, I happened to look over and see her handbag on the floor next to my foot. Her gun was inside.

I bit the inside of my cheek. The gun was right there. It was actually closer to me than it was to her. All I had to do was quickly lean forward and grab it, and we wouldn't have to fly to the jail in Pitchfork to break out Benedict Blackwood. I'd be a hero. I'd probably get to meet Sheriff Hoyt Graham. He might even pin an honorary deputy badge on my vest, once I bought a vest.

I was dreaming about how great it would be to be recognized as a hero when suddenly I heard a *THUMP*.

Egg!

I mean . . . Dorcas!

"I'm sorry, Rose," I said, slowly releasing her. "But I'm really tired, and I think I need to go to bed right now. I'll see you tomorrow."

"Alright," Rose said quietly as she wiped her eyes. "Thank you for listening and for being so kind. I want you to know that if I could, I would definitely let you and your parents go free. You're good people, and I really like you."

"Thanks," I said as I made my way back to the hallway.

But before I headed up the stairs to search for my missing aunt, I turned around and looked at Rose Blackwood, who was stuffing her handkerchief into her pocket.

"So why don't you?" I asked her. "Let us go, I mean. Why do you have to free your terrible brother from jail? You aren't a criminal, and I know you don't want to break the law by releasing a criminal. It doesn't even seem as though you like your family. And I don't think they deserve someone as nice as you. Maybe you can untie my parents, and the four of us can continue with this race. We could split the money afterwards. We could be a really great team."

"Believe me, W.B., I wish I could," Rose Blackwood said sadly, "but I have to free my brother. You're right, I don't like him. But he's my family. And my family is all that I have. My parents always told me I'd never amount to anything without them, and they're right. It's not like I can find a job someplace else. Who would want to hire the sister of Benedict Blackwood? That's why I can't let you and your parents go, and why I have to break him out of jail. I hope you understand. Goodnight, W.B."

And the funny thing was, I did sort of understand. My parents were weird and sometimes very annoying, but I would do anything for them. As I started to climb up the stairs I heard Rose Blackwood call out, "Alright, Dorcas! I'm coming up to check on you! Then we'll all get a couple hours of shut eye!"

Uh oh.

I didn't know if the pillows that I stuffed under Aunt Dorcas's blanket would be good enough to fool Rose. Rose wasn't stupid. Aunt Dorcas is the yappiest person in our family, and the fact that she'd been so quiet for so long must have seemed odd.

I ran down the hallway as I heard Rose Blackwood start up the stairs. When I got to Aunt Dorcas's room, I quickly threw open the door and turned on the kerosene lamp. The room was still empty. My aunt hadn't returned.

Then what was that thumping noise I heard earlier?

I heard Rose Blackwood reach the top of the staircase. I bit my lip as I looked around the room one more time, just to make sure my aunt wasn't hiding someplace that I had missed.

Rose's words echoed in my head. "If any of you tried to escape, I might be forced to do something terrible."

I looked in my Aunt Dorcas's closet, and then I had an idea. It was a slightly silly idea.

In fact, it was a very silly idea. A very silly and very

embarrassing idea. If anyone at school ever found out about it, I would never live it down.

I dimmed the kerosene lantern until the entire room was covered in shadows. Then I slipped on my aunt's poofy nightgown as well as her big, lacy bonnet, and quickly crawled into her fluffy bed and threw the covers over me. I was going to have to pretend to be Aunt Dorcas.

I felt like a marshmallow wrapped in a doily.

I'VE BEEN THINKING
ABOUT CHEESE ALL DAY

R ose Blackwood knocked on Aunt Dorcas's door.
It occurred to me that in addition to dressing like
her, I would also need to imitate my aunt's voice.

Great. As if I didn't already feel like a donkey's rear
end . . .

"Hmmmmmmmmm?" I hummed in a loud and high-
pitched tone.

I couldn't do a particularly good imitation of my aunt,
but I figured if I were loud enough it wouldn't really
matter. Rose Blackwood had only met Aunt Dorcas once
before, and all that she really remembered about her was
that she was annoying.

So when Rose opened the bedroom door, I immediately buried my face in my pillow and began to sob.

"Wooohooohooo booooohoooohooohooo!" I sobbed.

"Umm, Dorcas?" Rose said. "It's me. Rose. The kidnapper. Please don't cry."

"But I liiiiiike cryyyyiiiiiing!" I wept.

"Okay, then cry. Cry all you like. I just wanted to wish you goodnight, and also ask if I can get you anything to eat. Maybe a sandwich? Or some hot soup?"

"Nooooooo thank yooooouuuu!" I howled into my pillow, sobbing and crying and wailing with my entire body.

Wow. It really was exhausting to be so whiny and weepy. I couldn't understand how my Aunt Dorcas did it all the time.

"Alright, that's fine," Rose said, and I could hear her slowly backing out of the bedroom. "Don't worry though, I promise not to hurt you or anyone else in your family. You're all very kind people."

"I knoooooooooooooow. Thank yooouuuuuu."

"Goodnight, Dorcas. I'm just going to check on little W.B. now, and then I'll go to bed too. I'll see you tomorrow."

My heart dropped into my stomach. Then I burped, which blasted my heart into my throat. Then I cleared my throat, and my heart fell back down to where it was supposed to be in my chest. I can't scientifically prove that all of that happened inside of me, but it certainly felt like all of that happened when I heard Rose say that she was going to check my bedroom next. My *empty* bedroom.

Rose wasn't the genius that my parents were, but she wasn't a fool either. She knew that I had gone upstairs where there are only two rooms: my bedroom and Aunt Dorcas's. My parents' bedroom, the guest room, and the bathroom were all downstairs, which meant if I wasn't in my bedroom, then it was pretty obvious where I was.

As soon as I heard the door close, I slipped out of bed and went to the window. It was my only hope.

It was also one of my worst nightmares.

I slid open the window and looked outside. I could see the faint outline of the thin and wispy evening clouds below. There was no sound except for the cutting of the Baron Estate through the gentle night winds. My bedroom window was right next door, and it was open a crack. I always left my window open a crack at night so I'd get a nice breeze.

This was crazy. It was foolish. It was nuts. A little voice in my head told me that I should just walk out the door right now and confess to Rose Blackwood that Aunt

Dorcas was gone. Rose really did seem like a nice person. I could see why my parents trusted her.

I paused as I continued to lean my head out the window, looking at the two feet of empty space between Aunt Dorcas's window and my window.

"If any of you tried to escape, I might be forced to do something terrible."

Her words made me shiver. Rose did have a gun. She might not want to use it, but that didn't mean she wouldn't use it, especially if she felt like she didn't have any other choice.

Plus, there was another thought in my head, a thought that I know might sound really silly and stupid. Ever since I started keeping the secret about Aunt Dorcas, I had begun to feel sort of heroic, like I was doing something to help Sheriff Hoyt Graham in his fight against Benedict Blackwood. Maybe Aunt Dorcas had already returned to Pitchfork and told the sheriff about Rose Blackwood's plan. If that was the case, then what I needed to do was continue as though everything was normal. I *needed* to keep the secret. It was my patriotic duty.

I took a deep breath as I climbed out of Aunt Dorcas's window.

My arms and legs were covered in goosebumps as

I reached for my window ledge two feet away . . . AND MISSED!

I gasped. One of my slippers fell off my foot and landed somewhere in South Carolina. I was holding onto Aunt Dorcas's window ledge with one hand, hanging on with my tensed fingertips as my entire life flashed before my eyes. As a horribly cold wind blew up my nightgown, I saw everything that had happened to me from my birth to this very moment.

. . .

. . .

. . .

Wow. I really was the clumsiest person in the world. By my count, I had slipped, tripped, flipped, stumbled, bumbled, flopped, dropped, fell, was bonked on the head, poked in the eye, and had my nose tweaked over six thousand and twenty-eight times. That was a lot of clumsiness for a person to experience after only ten and a half years of living.

When my clumsy life stopped flashing before my eyes, I used all of my strength to reach up and catch the lip of Aunt Dorcas's window with my other hand. Then I started to swing my body back and forth, trying to build some momentum. When I had finally built enough, I reached out with my left hand and caught the bottom of my bedroom window. I quickly pulled myself up, climbed through the window, and flopped inside, landing quite gracefully on my head.

BONK.

That makes six thousand and twenty-nine times.

"W.B.!" Rose said loudly from the other side of the door. "What's going on? I hear flopping! And bonking! Open this door right now!"

I tried my best to catch my breath as I went to the door and opened it.

Rose Blackwood furrowed her brow as she stared at me quizzically. "That's what you sleep in?"

I looked down. I was still wearing Aunt Dorcas's bonnet and old-fashioned poofy nightgown, with fluffy sleeves, lace, and a large flower embroidered on the front.

"Yes," I said. "Yes, it is."

"Oh," Rose said, "alright then. Well, have a good night, W.B. And thank you again for listening to me earlier. It's nice to have someone to talk to about that sort of thing. Your parents said we'll be landing in Snortlebaum, Alabama shortly."

"Goodnight, Rose," I said to her as I climbed into bed.

"And . . ."

"And what?"

"And, well . . . I wanted you to know that just because your family doesn't understand and appreciate you, that doesn't mean that nobody will ever understand and appreciate you. You might not have found where you belong yet, but that doesn't mean that you don't belong somewhere."

Rose smiled. "Thanks, W.B. I really appreciate that. In fact, to thank your family for being so kind to me, I'm planning on cooking all of you a special breakfast tomorrow morning. What's your favorite breakfast food?"

"All of it. I've yet to meet a breakfast food that I don't like."

She laughed. "Alright. I'll make sure there's lots of everything. Oh, before I go to sleep I should ask your Aunt Dorcas what her favorite breakfast food is too. She seemed a bit upset, though not as upset as she was the first time I met her. Maybe a good breakfast will cheer her up. Goodnight, W.B."

Before I could tell her not to bother Aunt Dorcas again, Rose had already closed my door.

I sighed as I opened my bedroom window, hoping this would be the last time I had to climb out of it, but knowing almost certainly that it wouldn't be.

Snortlebaum, Alabama. Badgerknee, Arkansas. Grunch-ville, Kansas. Wubbawubba, Wyoming. Silleenaim, Idaho.

We passed through these towns in a blur, picking up all of the random items from the Hortense's Tooth Powder list. It almost seemed too easy. Because M and P kept drinking tea, they rarely slept; because they rarely slept, we rarely took any breaks. Soon we were so far ahead of everyone else that it seemed as though we could win the race with our eyes closed, though both Rose and I had to convince my parents that it wouldn't be a particularly good idea to try that.

I still spotted the sharp-nosed woman on the bicycle in every town we stopped at, and I still had no idea how she was following us. Maybe she had a rocket powered bicycle or something. Who knows? But since we continued ignoring each other, and I had enough to worry about without having to consider a person who I was pretending wasn't there in the first place, it didn't really seem to matter.

It wasn't until we reached Newer Oldtown, Nevada, or the place that we *thought* was Newer Oldtown, Nevada, that we had our first major problem on the ground.

M and P decided to take a much needed nap when we landed in the Nevada desert. They had been awake for days, and they were absolutely exhausted. Rose and I finished our breakfast of pancakes and fresh berries before we left the Baron Estate in order to fetch the next-to-last item from our list.

"Newer Oldtown Old Fashioned Beans," Rose said as she read from the list. "Yuck. I really hate baked beans. They're my least favorite food. Let's go, kiddo."

She tousled my hair and motioned for me to follow her.

Rose had started calling me kiddo and tousling my hair a lot, treating me more like a little brother than like someone she had kidnapped. She no longer held on to me like I was a prisoner when we walked through the towns, since she trusted me not to run away. She was being really nice to me, my parents, and Aunt Dorcas (or at least to the person who she thought was Aunt Dorcas, since it was really just me dressed in her nightgown), but she always carried her gun with her. Even when she cooked us all a big and delicious dinner, she did it with her gun tucked into her apron.

As we walked into town, I spotted the big wooden sign that welcomed us and told us how many people lived there. But it was so dirty and full of little, round holes that

I couldn't read what it said. It looked like this:

"Do you think woodpeckers did that?" I asked Rose, pointing to the holes.

"I don't know. Maybe. Or maybe it was termites," she answered. "Come on. Let's get these gross beans and then get out of here. I'd like to be in California before nightfall."

The town that we thought was Newer Oldtown was very different from the other towns we had visited. This was mostly because the other towns had people in them, and this town seemed to be completely empty. It looked like a ghost town, though I have to admit that if I was a ghost I wouldn't waste my time haunting such an ugly and rundown place. The gutters were overflowing with sludge and garbage, and most of the buildings looked like they were a hamster's sneeze away from toppling over. All of the windows were boarded up. A tumbleweed blew past us, and it wasn't one of those good looking tumbleweeds, either.

"Hello?" Rose called as we walked down the empty street.

She was answered by a loud *PING!*

"Ping?" I said with a frown.

"Yes, I heard that too," Rose said, then cupped her hands and called out, "Hello? Pinger?"

The pinger responded with another *PING!*

I noticed that the window across from us suddenly had a little round hole in it that it didn't have before. And it was about the same size as the holes in the town sign.

Suddenly, I understood the noise.

PING!

"Hello?" Rose called. "I can hear you, but I can't see you!"

"Rose, get down!" I cried, pulling Rose to the ground.

PING!

Suddenly there was another little hole in the wall where we'd been standing. Rose looked up and saw the hole, and I could see her brain finally make the connection.

"Ohhhhhh," she said, smacking herself on the forehead. "Ping! Now I get it. We're being shot at. Very clever of you to figure that out, W.B.! I'm proud of you."

"Gee, thanks."

PING! PING! PING!

Whoever was shooting at us was clearly enjoying it because they kept doing it without showing any signs of stopping. Rose and I crawled across the dirt road, coughing as we kicked dust in each other's faces. The pinging continued. Rose pointed to a building that looked like a hotel, and we quickly crawled inside.

We crawled through the lobby, up the stairs, down the hall, and all the way across a wide room that looked like a ballroom, until we realized that we probably didn't need to crawl anymore. So we stood up, dusted ourselves off, and found ourselves face-to-face with the ugliest and dirtiest group of men that I'd ever seen.

"Hello," said Rose to the ugly men. "My, what interesting faces you all have."

"Thank you," said one of the men as he stroked his chin, which looked like a twice baked potato. "What are you two doing here?"

"Hiding," I told him. "Someone was shooting at us."

"I know," said the man. "That was us."

One of the men, whose name we learned was Cletus, held up his gun and said, "Ping!"

Rose and I both raised our arms to show that we surrendered.

"Sir, we have no problem with you," said Rose. "We're just innocent travelers. Why are you shooting at us?"

The man with the potato chin spat on the ground. All of the other men spat as well. Rose spat too, and then nudged me in the ribs and gestured that I should do the same. I wasn't a particularly good spitter, so I just sneezed without covering my mouth instead.

"Bless you," said a man named Jud.

"Thank you."

"My name is Spud," said the man with the potato chin. "You two look like you come from that fancy town to the west. That lousy, no good, thieving town that thinks it's so much better than our town."

"No, we aren't from there," Rose said quickly. "We're from somewhere else, sir. We're just here to pick up some Newer Oldtown Old Fashioned Beans, then we'll be on our way. If you please, sir."

The ugly faces staring at us suddenly turned even uglier. Spud spat again. Jud sneezed.

"Bless you," I said.

"Thank you."

"Newer Oldtown?" Spud growled, looking like a rabid

dog on a bad hair day. "That's the town I was talking about! We *hate* them snooty Newer Oldtown folks. Those thieving liars think they're so high and mighty, with their fancy spoons, flowery soaps, custard-filled cakes, and underpants that don't stink. I wish every Newer Oldtown townsperson would jump off the edge of the earth!"

"Actually, that's not possible," I told him. "The earth is round. It doesn't have an edge. You can't jump off of it, no matter how hard you try."

The ugly men all looked down at the ground with frowns on their faces, and then looked back at me with even frownier frowns.

"Round?" asked Spud.

"But it looks flat to me," said Cletus.

"If it was round, then wouldn't we be falling all over the place?" asked Jud. "I mean, wouldn't the ground be rolling around under our feet like a billiard ball?"

"No," I said, suddenly remembering something my father had taught me. "Hand me that ball over there. I'll explain it to you."

Forty-five minutes later, after I'd explained gravity, the rotation of our planet, and the shape of the earth to the ugly men, they finally understood.

"Fascinating," said Spud as he scratched his chin. "So

that's why the sun comes up in the morning and goes down at night. It's because of the way that the planet is rotating and revolving around the sun. Huh. I always thought that the moon was just the sun's backside."

"I'm a little confused by what you said about time zones," said Cletus. "If Nevada is several hours behind New York, does that mean New York already knows what's happened today? Could we send a letter to them and ask what's going to happen in our future?"

"Could we travel back in time and meet our earlier selves? Maybe take ourselves out for an ice cream soda?" another ugly man asked. "I'm mighty lonely. I know I'd appreciate the pleasure of my company."

"Never mind that," Spud said, pulling out his gun again and pointing it at Rose and me. "As I said to you before, we *hate* them snooty Newer Oldtowners. This here is Older Newtown, Nevada. We've been fighting and feuding with Newer Oldtown ever since they stole our prized recipe for Older Newtown Old Fashioned Beans. Now they're making a fortune off those beans, when that money should be going to us!"

The rest of the ugly crew cried out, "Yeah!"

"I'm sorry, sir," said Rose. "We had no idea that they stole it from you. My nephew and I just wanted some beans. We'll gladly leave you alone now. Sorry to bother you. Have a lovely day."

As we turned to leave we heard the unmistakable sound of eleven gun triggers clicking, followed by a single squeak.

"Darnit, Carl! You've got to get that thing fixed!" Spud shouted to one of the men. "Your stupid squeaky gun just ruined the effect!"

Carl looked sadly at his rusty gun, which squeaked again as he shook it.

"You're not going anywhere," Spud told us.

"Oh, we aren't?" said Rose, her hand drifting slowly to the gun she had hidden in her bag.

But before she could grab her gun, her bag was suddenly snatched away by Carl and Jud. Carl pulled out Rose's gun, and Jud pulled out a used handkerchief.

"Trade you?" Jud said to Carl.

"Nope," said Carl, stuffing his squeaky gun in his holster as he examined Rose's black gun. "Say, this gun is pretty nice. I think I'll name it Harold, after my mom."

"Give that back!" Rose cried.

"Yeah, give it back!" I said.

And then I realized how stupid it was for a person to want their kidnapper to have her gun back.

"You're coming with us," said Spud. "We're on our way

to Newer Oldtown to tell them that they better give us back our beans, as well as all the money they've made off them. If they don't, then we'll be forced to fill them, and you two as well, with so many bullet holes that you'll look like Swiss cheese."

"I hate Swiss cheese," Rose moaned.

"Well, I can't think of a cleverer thing to say right now!" Spud snapped. "Now march! We're heading over to that snooty town right now."

Rose and I had no choice. We marched.

"You could have said that you'd fill them with so many holes that they'd whistle when the wind blew," Jud suggested to Spud.

Spud sighed.

"I guess. I'm just hungry, that's all. I've been thinking about cheese all day."

Luckily My Mouth Was Too Full of Muck

Rose and I were marched through the nearly empty town of Older Newtown. At first we marched with our hands up in the air to show that we were surrendering. When our arms got tired, we asked the men if we could put them down.

"Then how will we know you're surrendering to us?" Spud asked.

"We could remind you every couple of minutes?" I suggested.

They seemed to like that idea, so we continued the march with our arms hanging comfortably at our sides, and every few moments Rose and I would trade off saying, "I surrender!"

They marched us across the border of Newer Oldtown, where the city sign read:

WELCOME TO NEWER OLDTOWN,
NEVADA!
HOME OF THE ORIGINAL NEWER
OLDTOWN OLD FASHIONED BEANS!
ONLY AVAILABLE HERE!
POPULATION: 159,326 . . . AND
COUNTING!

"Lousy, snooty, no good thieving Newer Oldtowners," Jud muttered. "They think they're so high and mighty just because they can count that high."

"And there's nothing original about their beans either," Spud said. "These people make me sick to my stomach. Look at this place. Filled with frilly people in clothes without stains, restaurants that smell good, and I bet there aren't any snakes in their toilets either. They think they're so fancy and special."

"I surrender!" I chirped as I looked around the town.

It was actually the most beautiful town I'd ever seen. The people all looked so clean and well-dressed. It was as though we had managed to catch them on the day they all took their weekly bath. Everyone greeted us with a lovely smile and a wave. A man tipped his cap to Rose as he wished her good day.

"Good day to you too," Rose said. "I surrender!"

The busy streets were paved with cobblestone, and there were white horses pulling elaborately decorated carriages and men riding tall bicycles. Everywhere you looked, there were signs advertising Newer Oldtown Old Fashioned Beans. The signs were on buildings, on carriages, on fences, on horses, and one lady we passed had her baby wrapped in a Newer Oldtown Old Fashioned Beans blanket. Those beans were clearly something they were really proud of.

"I can't believe we've been kidnapped," Rose whispered to me.

"I can," I whispered back.

"What do you mean?"

"I mean, I'm already kidnapped," I whispered to her. "You already kidnapped me and my family. Now I've been kidnapped again, so I'm double-kidnapped."

"Oh."

"Yeah. Don't worry. You'll get used to it. I surrender!"

Spud, Jud, Cletus, Carl, and the rest of the ugly men marched us all the way to a large factory building with "Newer Oldtown Old Fashioned Beans" spelled out on the rooftop. The factory building smelled strongly of baked beans, which I happened to love. It made my mouth water. Then again, most food makes my mouth water. Maybe I just have a really watery mouth.

"Oh, gross," said Rose as she grimaced. "I think I'm going to be sick. I absolutely hate the stink of beans."

The ugly men looked at Rose as though she'd just slapped them in the face. A woman who was passing by with her children made an awful face at her, and her two children frowned as well. Apparently it was a crime to insult those beans.

"How dare you," Spud said to Rose. "What you're smelling is an Older Newtown recipe that dates back to the year 1770, when it was created by my great, great, great grandpappy, Skud P. Spuddlesworth, one of the greatest Americans to ever live in Nevada!"

"How is that possible?" I asked. "Nevada wasn't even a state until the year 1864. I think it belonged to Spain back in the 1700s."

"Wait, your name is Spud Spuddlesworth?" Rose asked with a giggle.

I coughed into my fist to hide my laughter.

Spud Spuddlesworth glared at us silently from beneath the brim of his bowler hat, which was riddled with holes.

"I hear a lot of silly babbling," he growled, "but I don't hear any surrendering."

"I surrender!" Rose and I declared at the same time.

The ugly gang led us into the Newer Oldtown Old Fashioned Beans Headquarters.

"Do you have an appointment?" asked the little man seated behind the front desk in the lobby.

All twelve of the ugly men pointed their guns at him.

"Well, do you?" the man repeated.

"No," said Jud. "Can we make one now?"

"Of course," said the man as he took out a large note-book. "What time would you like to make the appointment for?"

"Right now!" barked Spud.

"Alright. And what is the appointment about?"

"Us threatening whoever is in charge here," said Carl.

"Alright," said the man behind the desk as he jotted down a note in his notebook. "The president of the company, Mr. Bobby 'Best Beans' Kelly, is in a meeting right now, but he should be finished in about five minutes. Now if you'll just have a seat over there in the waiting room, I will call you when President Kelly is ready for you."

The dozen ugly men grumbled as they lowered their guns and sat down in the waiting room. Rose and I didn't know what to do, so we grumbled as well. I'm proud to say that I was the best grumbler there. It was probably because of all of the practice I'd had.

After five minutes of grumbling, the little man from the lobby told us we could go into President Kelly's office, which was located behind a large door at the end of the hall.

"I surrender!" Rose said as we all stepped inside the president of the company's office.

"You surrender to whom?" asked President "Best Beans" Kelly, a neatly dressed man sitting behind a gigantic desk.

The office of President Kelly was the fanciest room I'd ever been in. There were expensive looking oil paintings (of baked beans) and photographs (also of beans) and sculptures (of horses . . . just kidding, also of beans) all over the place. There were beautiful bookcases built into the wall behind his desk, but there were no books on the shelves, just cans of baked beans. It

was clear that only one thing mattered to President Kelly, and that thing was beans.

"They surrender to us!" Spud snapped at President Kelly. "And you will too, if you know what's good for you. We have a bone to pick with you!"

The threat did not seem to bother President Kelly. Instead he smiled and reached into the top drawer of his desk.

"You all look quite hungry. I know what you need," he said as he produced an open can of beans from his desk drawer. "You need a nice and tasty bite of Newer Oldtown Old Fashioned Beans. This should calm everyone down."

"You keep an open can of beans in your desk?" I asked.

"Of course. Who doesn't?"

"Gross . . ." Rose shuddered.

"Those aren't Newer Oldtown Old Fashioned Beans!" Spud spat. "Those are *Older Newtown* Old Fashioned Beans!"

President Kelly frowned as he stared at the can, reading the label.

"No, you're mistaken," he replied. "It says so right here. Newer Oldtown. But I can see why you'd make that mistake."

"Close the door," Spud said to me. "No one is getting out of here until we settle this."

I obeyed the ugly man and closed the door. As I closed it, I noticed the woman with the pointy nose and the bicycle standing in the lobby. She pretended that she didn't see me, so I pretended that I didn't see her either.

"Isn't anyone going to join me in a delicious can of beans?" President Kelly asked as he dug his spoon into the can. "How about you?" He turned to Rose, who shuddered again.

"No, thank you," she said. "I don't really like beans. But thank you for the offer."

President Kelly dropped his spoon. The twelve ugly men dropped their guns. My belt suddenly snapped, and I accidentally dropped my pants.

"You don't like beans?" President Kelly whispered in disbelief. "But . . . but everyone loves these beans. And I mean *everyone*."

"He's right," said Spud. "This special recipe dates back to the 1500s."

"You said it dated back to the 1700s," I told him.

"I did not! And pull your pants back up, kid!"

"I'm trying!"

President Kelly carried the can of beans over to Rose.

"I'm sorry, but I really don't like beans," Rose said as she tried to back away from President Kelly. "I've never liked them. Not even as a kid."

"But I bet you've never tried beans like this before," said

President "Best Beans" Kelly. "I guarantee you there isn't a finer bean in the world. Just give them a taste. You'll love them so much that you'll never want to eat anything else."

"Taste the beans," said Jud.

"You'll really love these beans," insisted Carl.

"They're the greatest beans in the world," said President Kelly.

"They're the greatest beans in the universe!" Spud declared.

All of the ugly men put down their weapons and opened cans of beans that they grabbed from the bookshelves. They dug their spoons into the cans and began moving towards Rose, who backed away while holding her hand over her mouth. The men seemed personally offended that Rose was not interested in tasting their prized beans. I offered to taste them for her, but everyone ignored me.

"Just try a little bite," Spud insisted. "What's the worst thing that could happen?"

"I could choke on them," Rose said as she backed into the door.

"Well, what's the second worst thing that could happen?"

"I could ruin my appetite for supper!"

Before any of the ugly men or the president could come

up with a response to that, the door was suddenly thrown open, knocking Rose Blackwood to the ground.

In stormed the gang of inventors.

The inventors had really changed since the beginning of the race, and I don't mean in a good way. Aside from behaving like criminals in order to win the contest (by robbing and destroying general stores, and attacking the Baron Estate like pirates in the sky), I noticed that the majority of them hadn't taken a bath or changed their clothes since the race had started. They all stank. Their white inventor coats were stained, and their goggles were fogged. They had stubble on their chins and their hair was so wild and greasy that it looked like octopi tentacles.

"Where are the beans?!" the inventors all shouted. Then they spotted the cans that were stacked on the bookshelves at the other end of the room.

"Alright," said the president of the company. "Just wait one moment, and I'll sell you each a can of Newer Old-town Old Fashioned Beans."

"You mean Older Newtown Old Fashioned Beans!" Spud snapped.

Before they could begin arguing over what the beans were really called, they were both trampled by the inventors who galloped across the room and began to fight over the cans, just as they had fought over every other item since the race had begun.

A single can dropped to the ground and rolled all the way across the room. I picked it up and stuck it into my pocket. Then I tugged at Rose's sleeve and motioned that we should leave. I could tell that things were about to get messy.

"Back away!" screamed Carl, as he pulled out Rose Blackwood's gun. "Get away from me, or I'll shoot!"

He was screaming at a group of inventors who were trying to use him as a stepladder to reach the beans located on the top shelf.

"Wait just a second," Rose said to me. She quickly scooted over to Carl, ducking as a mad scientist dove across the room to grab a crushed can of beans. "Carl!"

Carl spun around and pointed Rose's gun at Rose. "Yes?" he said.

"I wouldn't threaten people with my gun if I were you," she told him. "You should use your other gun."

"But that gun squeaks," Carl said with a pained look on his face. "Do you know how embarrassing it is to have a gun that squeaks? Nobody takes it seriously."

"That's unfortunate," Rose agreed, "but my gun is a single shooter. That means you can only fit one bullet in it at a time, and you can only fire it once. Look at all of these people here. They're going crazy over these beans. Don't you think you'll need more than a single shot?"

Carl looked around.

"Of course these beans are tasty!" Spud cried as an inventor stepped on his face. "They're made from a recipe discovered by my great-great-great-great-grandpappy back in the early 1200s!"

Two inventors jumped on Spud and wrestled his can from him. Most of the ugly men and the inventors had been thrown to the ground, and soon everyone was completely covered in beans. President "Best Beans" Kelly opened one of his larger desk drawers and locked himself inside. His assistant rushed in and asked the inventors if they had an appointment. One of them said that they did. The assistant checked his big book and saw that he was right, so he left the office and closed the door.

Carl handed the gun back to Rose. He took out his old rusty gun and began to wave it around.

"Alright!" Carl screamed to the inventors. "Everyone get down on the ground and put your hands up!"

Squeak! Carl's gun squeaked.

Rose and I snuck out of the office and ran back to the Baron Estate.

"W.B., you need to take a bath immediately," Rose told me after we'd taken off. "You stink like beans."

"So do you," I retorted.

Rose Blackwood smelled herself and gagged.

"Oh goodness . . . I smell even worse than you," she groaned. "Alright, I'll take a bath first, and then you can take one next."

"Sorry," said P. "No one will be taking a bath here. We're all out of water."

"If you like, you can go back to Newer Oldtown and have a bath," M suggested.

"No, thank you," Rose and I said at the same time.

"Alright," my mother said. "Well, then I suppose we should be moving on, shouldn't we? Next stop, Ruttleshlub, California. We should be there in about an hour."

"An hour?" Rose said, suddenly looking very excited. "And that's it, right? That's the last town we'll be going to? Then we'll head back to Chicago?"

"That's right!" P said triumphantly. "And we'll have won the race!"

P and M and Rose cheered.

I started to cheer too, but then I realized that as soon as we won the money, we'd be flying over to Pitchfork to free Benedict Blackwood. I didn't really feel like cheering after that.

We made the trip to California in less than one hour. Rose and I weren't able to take baths, so we sprayed each other with some of Aunt Dorcas's perfume in order to cover the bean stink. It didn't really help.

"Great," Rose Blackwood muttered. "Now I smell like a flower that's been rolled around in baked beans."

"It could be worse," I told her. "You could smell like those men from Older Newtown."

She thought for a moment before answering, "That's true."

The Baron Estate landed just outside of Ruttleshlub, California in the middle of a beautiful forest. The trees were exceptionally tall, with thick, red trunks and bright green leaves. The bushes were filled with brightly colored flowers, as well as delicious fruit, ripe for the picking. The air was lovely, and when Rose and I stepped outside we just stood there breathing for close to ten minutes. I had never been particularly interested in breathing before—I mean, I would regularly do it, but only so I wouldn't die. But this was the first time I ever really enjoyed doing it. Rose did, too.

"I could stand around breathing this air all day," she told me, "but we should probably get going if we want to beat those other inventors."

I agreed, and together we headed down the path leading to the town.

As we walked, I couldn't help but notice all of the animals along the way. There were frogs and lizards, deer and squirrels, chipmunks and rabbits, and tons of other animals that we could hear but couldn't see. The sky was full of happy and chirping birds. I looked down and saw two happy looking worms poke their heads out of two little holes in the ground. Or maybe the worms were poking their backsides out of the holes. It's hard to tell which side is which with worms. I bet they can't tell the difference either. Still, they looked happy.

Suddenly we heard a loud snorting sound from deeper within the forest. It frightened the animals terribly, and they all quickly ran and scuttled and scampered and slithered to safety, hiding under rocks, under bushes, up in the trees, and underground. Rose and I looked at each other and shrugged.

Soon we reached the town sign welcoming us to Ruttleshlub.

WELCOME TO
RUTTLESHLUB, CALIFORNIA.
HUMAN POPULATION: 142,000
WILD PIG POPULATION: 161,000

"Isn't that odd? Why would they bother counting the wild pigs?" I asked Rose.

"I don't know," Rose answered. "Maybe they were bored."

Once we reached the town we started to look around for some sort of general store or shop where we could find the last item on our list. Suddenly, a man who was moving very quickly crashed into Rose, knocking her to the ground.

"Oh, oh dear, I'm so sorry," the man apologized, tipping his hat to her. "Are you all right, Miss?"

Rose slowly stood up and dusted herself off. "Yes, I suppose," she said. "But you should watch where you're going next time. You got dirt in my hair."

The man frowned as he inspected her hair.

"Oh dear, you're right. And I've somehow made you smell like old baked beans as well. I'm terribly, terribly, terribly sorry. Please forgive me. Here, let me make it up to you."

He reached into the large basket he was carrying and pulled out a bottle.

"What is that?" Rose asked.

"Ruttleshlub Hair Tonic," the man said proudly. "Just put a little splash of it on your head, and your hair will be stronger and fuller and cleaner than you ever imagined it could be. I used to have a shop that sold this wonderful tonic, but that shop closed this morning. So now I sell it door-to-door. I usually charge twenty-five-and-a-half cents for it, but because I knocked you over, I'm willing to give it to you for only twenty-five! What a deal, right? In fact, it's such a great deal that you can't afford *not* to buy it!"

Rose's eyes widened as she looked at the list in her hand.

The last item we had to collect was Ruttleshlub Hair Tonic. And then we were finished with the race.

"Kiddo, pay the man." Rose instructed.

I gave the salesman my last twenty-five cents, and he handed over the hair tonic.

"Have a lovely day!" the man chirped, tipping his cap and then scurrying further down the path where he promptly knocked over another lady.

"Oh, oh dear, I'm so sorry," we heard the salesman apologize to the woman as he helped her up out of the dirt. "Are you all right, Miss? Oh dear. It appears I've gotten your hair dirty. Here, let me make it up to you. Have you heard of Ruttleshlub Hair Tonic?"

Rose handed me the bottle and gave me a huge hug. "We've got it! Now all we have to do is get back to Chicago, and we've won!"

She started to do a little dance, and, because I was excited too, I did a little dance as well.

"Goodness! I believe these two people have bees in their trousers!" cried an elderly woman who was passing by.

We decided to stop dancing after that.

We were skipping back along the path that would lead us to the Baron Estate, and feeling as though we were on top of the world.

"The other inventors won't be able to find the hair tonic in a shop!" Rose told me with a gleeful smile. "They'll need to find that salesman! It'll take them forever to catch up to us! We've won! We've won!"

"Don't count your chickens before they've hatched," I warned her. "Sure it seems like we've won, but you never know when something bad might happen. We must be very careful, because if we're not, we—"

Before I could finish my sentence, I stumbled over a rock and began to tumble down a rocky hill. I bounced all the way down, landing hard on each and every rock. When I finally hit the bottom, the bottle of hair tonic flew out of my hands.

"W.B.!" Rose cried. She immediately began to rush down the hill after me.

I was dizzy from my long and painful fall, but I was determined not to let that bottle of hair tonic break. So I quickly stood up and dove forward, catching the bottle with one hand just before it landed on one of the large, pig shaped stones surrounding me at the bottom of the hill

"Good catch, kiddo!" Rose cried as she pumped her fist in the air.

I stood there with the bottle in my hand and posed triumphantly. I had never caught anything before. I always dropped everything, and I mean *everything*: bottles, plates, trays, pitchers, cans, jars, boxes, beakers, books, babies—you name it, and I've dropped it. But I caught the bottle of hair tonic, which was by far the most important thing I'd ever had to catch. Maybe this was the start of a new W.B., of a kid who no longer tripped, slipped, and bonked his head every five minutes. Maybe I was finally finding some good luck.

Then one of the pig shaped stones sniffed the air and snorted. It opened its eyes and looked at me.

"Uh oh."

I heard another snort, followed by another one, and yet another. Soon I was surrounded by snorts, and it finally occurred to me that I had landed in a wild pig pen.

I was surrounded by hungry wild pigs . . . and I smelled strongly like the most delicious baked beans in the universe.

Rose screamed, "W.B.! Run!"

This brings us back to the pig incident which, as I told you, involves me lying face down in the mud. Luckily for me, the bottle of hair tonic didn't break when I tripped and fell. Unluckily for me, the pigs were about to squish me into gravy. So I guess that sort of cancels out.

I attempted to stand, but I slipped and fell back into the muck. Using my sleeve to wipe the mud from my eyes, I turned back and saw the wild pigs as they raced down the path, about to treat me in the same cruel way that I'd been treating bacon for all my life. Suddenly, I heard a loud *BANG!*

The wild pigs all squealed and immediately turned in the opposite direction and began to run away. I looked back at the Baron Estate and saw Rose Blackwood standing there with her smoking gun in her hand. She'd fired a shot into the air.

"Come on, W.B., you can finish your mud bath when we get to Chicago," she quipped.

I had something mean that I was going to say back to her, but luckily my mouth was too full of muck.

You Showed the Whole Country Your Bloomers for Nothing

We still didn't have any water, but we had plenty of orange juice, so I decided to try an orange juice bath to wash some of the mud off. I don't recommend taking an orange juice bath. For one thing, it made me really sticky. Everything that I touched afterwards stuck to me. At one point, I slipped coming down the stairs and Rose Blackwood had to peel me off the ground.

"At least you don't smell like beans anymore," she said with a smile.

"Nope. I just smell like a rotten fruit salad," I joked, and we both laughed.

"Listen, Rose," I continued, "I want to thank you for saving my life when you fired your gun and frightened the wild pigs. I remember what you said to Carl when you convinced him to return your gun during the battle at the bean factory. You gave up your only bullet to save me, didn't you?"

Rose's smile flickered. She looked at me with uncertainty in her eyes as she opened her mouth, and then closed it. I could see her having an internal argument with herself about whether or not to tell me the truth about her gun and its bullets, an argument which I could see was finally settled as she sighed and rolled her eyes. She looked like a kid who had just been caught in a lie, but was ultimately grateful that she wouldn't have to keep up the lie anymore. She seemed both frightened and relieved. I could understand that.

At that moment I knew that I could trust Rose Blackwood.

"Yes, I did," she said slowly. "It's true. You and your family have treated me so well. I wouldn't have been able to forgive myself if I didn't help you. Plus, I know you would have done the same for me."

And she was right. I would have, and so would my parents. Though we began our journey as kidnapper and kidnapped, Rose had somehow managed to fit into my strange family in a way that no one else ever had before. I felt comfortable with her, like I had known her all of my life. And I no longer resented her for what she was doing because I could see that she was only doing it because she was a loyal person. She would have done the same for me if I were the one locked up in the Pitchfork jailhouse.

With all ten items in our possession, we were making our victory lap to Chicago. We were all too excited to rest, so we gathered together in the garage and watched as my parents flew the magnificent flying Baron Estate to victory. We flew over the California border and into Nevada— which, to tell you the truth, still smelled like beans to me— then we passed over Utah Territory—which didn't really smell like anything—and then crossed the towering mountains of Colorado Territory. I had never seen anything as large and beautiful as the Rocky Mountains; I started to wonder if my parents and I could fly the Baron Estate there for a little family vacation once we'd finished the race. The peaks were all tipped with white snow. I wondered if it was as soft and fluffy as it looked.

"This is wonderful. We're almost there. You know what? Aunt Dorcas should be here with us to experience this lovely moment," M said as she continued to guide my father to Chicago.

My stomach flipped.

"Why would we get Aunt Dorcas? Are things too quiet and pleasant for you right now?" P asked.

"McLaron. She's my sister. I want to celebrate with her."

"I'll go get her," Rose said.

I quickly sprung up, tripped over my shoelaces, and then landed hard on my face. Rose used the end of a broomstick to peel my face off the ground, and then she helped me onto my feet.

"I'll do it," I said. "I mean, I'll ask her if she wants to come down. You can all just stay here and enjoy the view."

Rose thanked me and added, "And since we're almost there, and since you've all been so wonderful to me, I think I'll untie your parents a bit early."

"Oh, that's alright dear. We don't want to be a bother," said my mother.

"You don't have to do that if you don't feel comfortable with us being free," my father said, and then he began to spin. "Wheeee!"

"I insist," Rose said. "Thank you all for your help and kindness. I'll never forget what you did for me."

As she began to untie my mother and my father, I left

the garage and made my way up the staircase.

I hadn't given up my search for Aunt Dorcas. I still heard strange things at night, bumps and creaks, and once I heard a strange knocking noise that sounded as though it had come from outside. That could have been the result of the winds, the machinery that was helping to fly the house, or maybe it was a duck that just wanted to visit. I wasn't sure.

I went into Aunt Dorcas's room, which, of course, was empty. I pretended to have a conversation with her, speaking loudly in my voice, and then answering in a high-pitched voice in case anyone downstairs was listening. When I felt enough time had passed, I returned to the garage where my father was allowing Rose Blackwood to steer the Baron Estate.

"There you go! You're a natural!" my father exclaimed. "What a great student you are. In fact, here."

He reached into his pocket and pulled out a nifty cap. He put it on Rose's head. It said "FIRST MATE" on it.

"Gosh, thanks, Mr. Baron," said Rose as she blushed. "I've never been 'First' anything before."

"Aunt Dorcas is tired," I interrupted. "She wants to finish taking her nap. She's still complaining about her knee."

"Careful. You want to avoid those winds up ahead. And also that big group of ducks," my mother warned Rose.

"What group of ducks?" Rose asked.

THUMP! THUMP! THUMP! THUMP!

"Never mind."

Rose, who really was quite good at flying the Baron Estate, flew us all the way back to Chicago. There was a huge crowd waiting for us at the Grand Exposition Fairgrounds, much larger than the crowd that had seen us off. It was a large celebration, larger than anything I'd ever seen before. There were musicians and jugglers and dancers and clowns and fire breathers and men on stilts, as well as people selling candy and cakes and pies and popcorn. I pressed my face to the window and watched with a huge smile as Rose began to lower the Baron Estate to the ground. She landed it smoothly and my parents both applauded her. Rose blushed as she curtsied, clearly not used to being applauded or appreciated.

I peeled my sticky face from the window, and we all rushed out of the garage to the front door.

"This is so very exciting!" said M.

"We'll probably get our picture in the paper!" I said.

"I wonder if they'll give us the money in cash or as a check," Rose commented.

"Wait, where's my horse?" P asked.

M opened the front door and all four of us posed proudly, expecting a hundred different people to be taking our picture.

Instead, there were sixteen deputy officers of the law standing there. They each had badges on their vests and guns in their hands.

"Alright, Rose Blackwood!" one of the deputy officers said. "Come on out with your hands up! We've got your floating house surrounded!"

"*Flying* house," my father corrected.

Rose, who looked absolutely dumbstruck, quickly reached into her bag and pulled out her gun. She pointed it at the sixteen deputy officers who all immediately lowered their weapons. I noticed that Rose's hand was shaking.

"Hold on," one of the officers said as he held up his hands. "Don't do anything stupid, Rose. Let the Baron family go."

"No!" shouted Rose. "In fact, I think we're going to leave. Mr. and Mrs. Baron, go back to the garage. We're flying out of here right now!"

As M and P snapped salutes and prepared to return to the work garage, they were interrupted by a very familiar shrieking voice. It was a voice that none of us had heard in quite some time.

"Wait! Wait! Waaaaiiit!"

The voice appeared to be coming from under the Baron Estate. I looked down at the base of our house and saw the filthy head of Aunt Dorcas poke out from the crawl space. Her hair was a giant, poofy nest with sticks and twigs stuck in it. She looked as though she had just survived a dozen hurricanes. My aunt crawled out from under the house and stumbled over to the deputy officers.

"Don't listen to her threats!" Aunt Dorcas roared. "That gun she is carrying has no bullets! She fired her only bullet back in California. Arrest her!"

I watched as the color left Rose Blackwood's face. It was true. She had told Carl that her gun only held one bullet, and she had fired it to scare the wild pigs away from me when I was flopping in the mud. And she had confirmed to me that it was the truth.

"It's true!" another voice under the house declared. "I heard her say so!"

I watched in shock as the sharp-nosed woman crawled out from under the Baron Estate, pushing her bicycle in front of her. I slapped myself on the forehead when I realized that the reason why she was able to travel so quickly was because she was actually travelling *with us*.

And then I regretted slapping my forehead, not only because it hurt, but also because my hand was now stuck to my forehead, and I couldn't get it off.

"Dorcas? What are you doing under the house? Who is that woman?" my mother asked, looking incredibly confused.

"My name is Cutty, and I work with the state of Massachusetts sheriff's department," the sharp-nosed woman said. She reached into the basket of her bicycle and showed my mother a badge before continuing, "I've been traveling with Dorcas to make sure that Rose Blackwood wouldn't hurt little Waldo Baron. We've been living underneath the house and also in the walls. I was waiting for the opportunity to take Rose's gun away, but every time I tried, your son would stumble or fall and hurt himself. He is, quite possibly, the clumsiest boy in all of America."

All eyes went to me. I tried to wave to everyone, but my right hand was still stuck to my forehead. I tried to pull my right hand off my forehead with my left hand, but then those two hands got stuck together, so I just stopped trying.

"How long have you been under the house?" Rose

Blackwood asked Aunt Dorcas.

"Since the very beginning!" Aunt Dorcas bellowed. "The first thing I did when that awful woman captured us was sneak out of my window and hide underneath the house. Then I tied all of my bloomers together and used my talent for sewing to stitch a message across them stating that we were kidnapped by the horrible Rose Blackwood. I hung that message from the bottom of the house. I imagine these Chicago deputies spotted the message, which is why they're here."

"That's true, ma'am," one of the deputies confirmed as he tipped his hat to my aunt. "Thank you for the help."

Aunt Dorcas continued, "Miss Cutty saw my message while we were flying over Massachusetts. She snuck under the house with me, and we've been waiting for the opportunity to capture Rose Blackwood ever since! Which we did, thanks to my bloomers!"

Everyone cheered, except for Rose, my mother, my father, and me.

The officers slipped handcuffs over Rose's wrists. Rose looked over and saw a long string of dirty bloomers attached to the bottom of the house.

"But I don't understand," she said. "I saw you in your bedroom, Dorcas. We talked to each other. Several times."

"That was actually the young Baron boy in disguise," said Miss Cutty. "Despite the fact that he's incredibly clumsy, he was actually quite clever and brave. If it hadn't been for him, Rose would have noticed that Dorcas was missing."

Everyone cheered again. Several people even began to chant my name. But I was as miserable as I'd ever been. Rose Blackwood looked at me in shock, as though she couldn't believe that I would actually betray her. I had to look away. It was true that she had kidnapped us . . . but I still felt really bad for her.

I tried to peel my hands from my forehead again.

The man with the banana cart suddenly rushed onto the fairgrounds. He had all ten items from the list.

"Aw, nuts!" he cried when he spotted us. "I was so close!"

"Rose Blackwood, you are under arrest," a deputy stated.

"Justice will now be served!" Aunt Dorcas cried triumphantly. "And we've also won the race! That's why I put up with being trapped under an awful flying house! I told Miss Cutty that my family needed to finish the race. And now the five hundred dollars is ours! Hooray!"

As if on cue, one of the men from Hortense's Tooth

Powder cleared his throat and walked over to us. He had a very serious expression on his face. The entire crowd went silent as he climbed the front steps to the Baron Estate.

"I'm afraid that you have been disqualified," he told us. "You were helped by a criminal, which goes against the rules. You aren't allowed to break any laws or associate with criminals while participating in the race. You have lost. Giving you five hundred dollars would ruin the good name of Hortense's Tooth Powder."

"*Hor-tense!*" the other Hortense's Tooth Powder men sang brightly as they waved their hands in a jazzy manner.

My family all gasped at the same time. And even though she probably hated us, especially me, Rose gasped as well. It didn't seem fair. We had collected all the items the fastest, and we were the only ones to do so without resorting to theft or criminal behavior. The other inventors had broken dozens of laws, yet we were the ones being punished.

The audience was in shock, too. They were so shocked that they had fallen silent. The only person who wasn't quiet was the man with the banana cart, who broke out into a joyful song and dance when he realized that he had just won five hundred dollars.

"We lost . . ." Aunt Dorcas choked as she dropped to

her knees. "All that . . . I went through all of that . . . and we still lost. Do you know what this means?"

"Yes," I said as I finally unstuck my hands and patted my aunt on the back. "It means you showed the whole country your bloomers for nothing."

ABOUT THE ANGRY
CHICKEN THING . . .

We stopped at a hotel in Chicago so we could clean up and change our clothes. I no longer smelled like beans or oranges, but after I had cleaned the rest of the dirt off me, I saw how bruised my entire body was. I looked like a blueberry. That's probably what Shorty would have called me if she could see me. At first I couldn't believe it, but then I counted all of the times I'd tripped, stumbled, tumbled, been poked, and was bonked on the head over the past week, and I was actually surprised that I didn't look worse.

Aunt Dorcas was upset about us not winning the money, so she locked herself in her bedroom. She said she didn't want to see anyone or talk to anyone. We were all grateful for that.

"Maybe we can win the next race around the country," M said.

"Or maybe a race around the world?" P replied. "That could be a lot of fun."

But I could tell from their sad expressions that they had lost their enthusiasm for racing. In fact, I wouldn't be surprised if they never attempted another race or flying adventure again. Strangely enough, the thought made me really sad.

As my parents prepared to fly the Baron Estate back home, there was a knock at our door. M answered it. Standing on our doorstep were the deputy officers. They were positioned in a circle around Rose Blackwood, who was in handcuffs.

"Excuse me, ma'am," a deputy officer said to my mother as he tipped his hat, "but we were wondering . . . can we catch a ride to Pitchfork? We understand that Rose's brother Benedict is being held there. The governor here has decided that Rose should have her trial in Pitchfork as well."

"Well, that's fine by me. But does she really need to wear those handcuffs?" M asked.

"Yes, ma'am," all the deputies said at once.

"It's alright, Mrs. Baron," Rose said quietly. "I don't mind."

I could tell by her expression that M was very unhappy

about that, but she wasn't the sort of person who would argue with officers of the law.

"Alright then," M said. "But everyone wipe your feet before you come inside."

The deputies sat in the living room with Rose Blackwood. I hid in the hallway and stole glances at her. I wanted to see Rose, but at the same time I really didn't want her to see me. She had saved my life by using her only bullet when I was about to be attacked by wild pigs, and I had betrayed her by lying about Aunt Dorcas. But then again, she had also kidnapped me and my family. It was all so confusing, and thinking about it made me feel like my brain was twisting itself into a butterfly knot.

I tried to talk to my father about it, but the moment I stepped into the garage he slapped a silly cap on my head that said "SECOND MATE" on it. I told him that I didn't want to be second mate. I just wanted to talk to him. Then he took that cap away and slapped an even sillier one on my head that said "THIRD MATE."

I stopped trying to talk to my father after that.

I asked my mother if I should feel bad about Rose going to jail, and her response confused me even more.

"W.B.," she started as she shoveled coal into the furnace, "I can't tell you what you should feel about Rose. Only you can decide that."

We arrived in downtown Pitchfork later that afternoon, and for a moment I forgot all about Rose and my jumbled feelings about her arrest. I was finally here, in the center of the town from all of my favorite stories. Yes, I had missed Sheriff Hoyt Graham's show last week, but maybe this would be even better. I would be able to meet my hero, shake his hand, and let him know that I had played an important part in capturing Benedict Blackwood's sister.

I have to say that the town of Pitchfork was not exactly how I imagined it. I pictured a Wild West town with busy and bustling streets, and the sheriff and his deputies riding around on their horses, their badges shining brightly in the sun. In my mind, everything and everyone was clean and lawful and orderly, sort of like Newer Oldtown, but without the beans. That's what all of the pictures in Sheriff Graham's books showed, but that wasn't what we found when we opened the front door to the Baron Estate and looked outside.

PING! PING! PING!

Rose and I ducked. The deputies and my parents looked around confused.

"Ping?" said my mother.

"Everybody get down!" Rose cried. "Someone is shooting at us!"

For a moment no one believed her. And then one of the deputy officer's hats was shot off his head.

PING!

They all dropped to the floor and closed the door as the bullets continued to fly towards the Baron Estate. We looked out the window and saw dozens and dozens of masked bandits running through the town, firing their guns and cackling madly.

"What's happening?" shouted one of the deputy officers. "This is Pitchfork! It's run by Sheriff Hoyt Graham and his deputies."

Another deputy officer went to the window and

opened it. There was a dangerous looking paperboy standing on the street corner selling newspapers and pocketknives. The officer waved him over to the window.

"Whadda ya want?" the paperboy snarled at the deputy officer.

The deputy asked, "What's happening here? There's crime everywhere!"

"Buy a paper to find out," the kid snapped. "Otherwise don't waste my time."

The deputy grumbled as he pulled a few pennies from his pocket and handed them to the kid. The kid gave the deputy a paper, but not before stealing his watch, his wallet, and his gun.

We all gathered around the newspaper to read as the gunshots from outside battered the Baron Estate like hail.

World famous bandit Benedict Blackwood has escaped after Sheriff Hoyt Graham was knocked unconscious by a falling fountain pen. He has taken control of the town and declared himself the king of Arizona Territory. He claims that everyone who does not bow to him will be tied to his horse and dragged across a cactus field.

ALL HAIL KING BENEDICT!

My parents looked at me in horror, and for a moment I didn't understand why.

But then I remembered something that had happened several days ago, on the first day that I learned my parents had turned our home into a flying machine.

"May I please borrow your pen, P?" I asked.

"Yes, of course."

He handed me the pen. Without a word, I turned and threw it out the open door.

"We are flying," I repeated to my father. "That is why your pen is now falling several hundred feet back to earth. Why are we flying?"

"Oh dear, I hope that pen doesn't hit anyone," M said.

It was my fault.

I hit Sheriff Graham with the pen.

Maybe I *am* cursed.

"What should we do?" M asked the deputies.

"Well," said one of the deputy officers, "I don't know about everyone else, but I'm a coward. And as a coward, I believe we should fly far, far, away from all of this. I've heard Brazil is lovely this time of year. Let's go there."

Another officer voiced his agreement. "I admit, I'm also

a coward. And a bit of a whiner. If anyone insists we stay, I'm going to whine and complain about it."

"I'm not a coward!" another deputy argued. "I want to stay here and fight!"

Several deputies agreed.

"But I don't wanna!" the whiney deputy whined.

"Let's take a vote," suggested another.

They took a quick vote to see who was in favor of staying and who was in favor of running away. It was a tie.

Suddenly there was a loud crashing noise. One of the criminals had thrown a brick through the living room window. We could now hear even more gunfire. There was someone pounding on the front door and someone else pounding on the backdoor. We heard an explosion, followed by another one that was even louder. Bandits were rolling barrels filled with gunpowder into buildings and then setting them on fire. Half of the shops on the block

were going up in flames. Pitchfork was falling apart.

We took another quick vote.

This time, we all voted in favor of running away.

P and M rushed to the garage to start up the Baron Estate while I sat there with the deputy officers and Rose Blackwood.

"I'm sorry I lied to you," I said to Rose. "I was just trying to protect my family."

"I know. I'm not mad at you," she said.

"You're not?"

She shook her head.

There was another explosion from outside, and this one shook the entire Baron Estate. The rest of our pictures fell off the walls and the bookshelves toppled over too. I heard the horrible cuckoo clock in the garage fall and cuckoo its last cuckoo.

"Oh, thank goodness," I muttered. "I thought that thing would never die."

"I hope we get out of here soon," said one of the deputy officers through chattering teeth. "I've heard horrible things about what Benedict Blackwood does to the people he captures. I heard he once punched a man so hard, his face spun around to the back of his head."

"I heard he doesn't even carry a gun. I heard he just

pours the bullets into his mouth and spits them at you. His burps are said to be deadly," another deputy added.

"I heard that he eats an entire cow for breakfast every morning."

"I heard that he sleeps on a bed of hot coals."

"I heard that his beard is made of rusty nails."

"I heard that his mother was a bull and his father was a barrel of gunpowder."

The deputies were discussing the rumors about Benedict Blackwood so intently, that they didn't hear my mother and father come back into the living room.

"Everyone?" P said gravely.

The deputies continued to talk.

"Deputies?" M said.

The deputies ignored her.

"Ping!" I shouted.

Everyone ducked. The deputies finally turned their attention to my parents.

P thanked me. "Well, I have some good news, and I have some bad news. Which would everyone like to hear first?" he asked.

We all gathered together and took a vote by raising our hands. The deputies took off Rose's handcuffs so she could participate in the vote as well.

Bad news narrowly beat out good news by a single vote.

"We want to know the bad news first," Rose told my parents.

"The bad news is . . . the Baron Estate has been damaged by the gunfire and explosions. We can't fly. We're trapped here until it can be repaired." P explained.

We all trembled in fear. Being trapped in a town run by Benedict Blackwood without Sheriff Hoyt Graham meant we were all in terrible danger.

"What's the good news?" I asked.

P cleared his throat and wiped the sweat from his forehead.

"The good news," P said, "is that the weather here is quite lovely. Normally Pitchfork is really hot and dry, but there's actually a really nice breeze. We felt it in the garage after a masked bandit threw a rock through our window. It also looks like rain, which will be good for all of the local plant life."

Suddenly, the front door to the Baron Estate was kicked open. The wood splintered into a thousand pieces from the force of the kick. We all froze in place, our voices trapped in our throats. What we saw standing in front of us was the most terrifying sight that we had ever seen.

But my father was right. The weather outside was quite

lovely.

"Well, well, well," chortled King Benedict Blackwood as he adjusted his crown with the end of his gun. "If it isn't my worthless little sister, Rose. Have you finally gotten yourself arrested? I'm proud of you."

He was just as I had imagined him, tall and hairy, with arms so big and muscular that he needed to turn sideways in order to fit through the doorway.

"I'm not proud of myself," Rose said bitterly. "I'm ashamed. This has been the worst week of my life. I can't believe you actually enjoy doing this. You should be locked away for a million years, you villainous creep. I wish I had never tried to free you . . ."

"Sticks and stones will break people's bones, so that's why I always carry them with me," Benedict replied.

"I don't think that's how that saying goes," said one of the deputies. "Isn't it 'sticks and stones may break my bones, but words will—'"

Before the deputy could finish the saying, King Benedict took a stick and threw it at him, breaking several of his bones. Then he took out another stick and pointed it at the rest of us.

"Does anyone else feel like correcting me?" the king barked.

We all shook our heads.

The king ordered his men to tie us up, which they did with glee. They also robbed us, stealing our pocket money, our watches, M and P's glasses, the deputies' guns, and my silly looking third mate cap.

"Hah!" said the robber as he placed the cap on his greasy head. "How do you like this, kid? I've got your cap! I bet you want it back, don't you?"

"No. It actually looks better on you. Keep it."

The robber frowned. "But I bet you'll cry yourself to sleep over losing this precious cap," he said to me. He ran his fingers over the abnormally wide brim. "I bet it'll haunt your dreams forever. You'll miss this cap terribly!"

"No. Actually, I forgot that I was even wearing it. It's not really my style. It's all yours."

The robber frowned and skulked away while muttering how I wasn't making the robbery very fun.

The rest of the robbers began to search through the house, stealing everything they could find that looked valuable. They started with clocks, silverware, and fancy plates, before moving on to some of my parents' strange inventions. One man tried to steal a tooth brushing machine, but when he tried to stick it in the sack he'd slung over his back, it jumped out and started violently brushing his

teeth. The man panicked and began to punch the machine, which only made it brush him harder. Several of the other robbers tried to pull the tooth brushing machine off of him, but then it started brushing their teeth as well. Soon all of the robbers had freshly cleaned teeth.

After that, they decided to leave the inventions alone.

Benedict Blackwood walked up the stairs of the Baron Estate, stealing all the picture frames from the walls. He reached the top of the staircase and began to travel down the hall.

"Oh no," M muttered. "Poor Aunt Dorcas."

Suddenly we heard a loud squawk, followed by a

loud squeal, followed by an explosion of sobs, blubbers, screeches, screams, cries, whines, and every other unpleasant high noise you can imagine hearing an eggy aunt make.

Benedict Blackwood rushed down the stairs with his hands over his ears. "Alright, men!" he shouted. "We're taking these prisoners along with us. We're going to lock them in the city jail. That's an order from your king!"

"Yes, Your Majesty!" the robbers cried, saluting their king.

"What about that lady upstairs? Shouldn't we tie her up and take her with us too?" one of the robbers asked.

"No!" Benedict Blackwood said quickly. "I don't want that woman anywhere near me. Listening to her is like having an angry chicken trapped in your brain."

"Hey, I had the same thought about her!" I told him. I felt every evil eye in the room turn to me. "I mean, about the angry chicken thing . . ."

A HUNDRED HORSES
SNORTING ALL AT ONCE

The newly crowned King Benedict Blackwood had made his mark on the town of Pitchfork. On top of legalizing crime, he had closed all the shops and restaurants that he didn't like and turned them into giant outhouses. If you don't know what an outhouse is, consider yourself lucky. If you do, then you can imagine what the town smelled like now.

The weather in Pitchfork was apparently in tune with our mood. The lovely temperature P had raved about turned sour in an instant. A heavy rain began to fall as we were led from the Baron Estate to the Pitchfork jail down the street. We trudged through heavy mud and muck. I walked beside Rose Blackwood and tried to catch her eye, but she wouldn't look up at me. She just kept staring at the toes of her boots with her shoulders slumped in defeat. I had never seen anyone look so sad and ashamed before.

Suddenly, I felt so terrible for Rose that I did something very foolish.

"Excuse me?" I said to Benedict Blackwood, who was leading us to the jail. "Mr. King Blackwood, sir? I think you should let Rose go."

The criminals walking beside us froze with their mouths wide open. They couldn't believe that someone would actually dare to tell the King of Arizona Territory what to do.

Benedict Blackwood turned to me with an amused expression on his face.

"What was that, pipsqueak?" he asked. "I don't think I heard you correctly."

"I said you should let Rose go," I told him.

"W.B., please, don't—" Rose began, but then one of the criminals wrapped a gag around her mouth, silencing her.

"And why should I do that?" Benedicts asked me, taking a knife from his pocket and sharpening it against his scruffy chin.

"Because she was coming here to free you from jail. She kidnapped me and my family. She was going to rob us and force us to bring her here in our floating home to break you out of jail."

"It's not a floating home. That's clearly a flying home, pipsqueak. A floating home would be a home that just rises up in the air without you being able to control it, like a regular balloon. A flying home is a home that you can control, like a hot air balloon," Benedict informed me.

"Thank you!" my father said in an exasperated tone. "It's really not so hard to understand, W.B."

"But she was willing to break the law to save you," I told Benedict Blackwood, suddenly feeling angrier than I'd ever felt before. "She hates breaking the law, but she was willing to do it because you're her family. And now you're just going to throw her in jail?"

"Well, yes, I am," said Benedict Blackwood with a chuckle. "I've never liked Rose. No one in our family does. She's not like us, and she never will be."

"Well . . . then you're . . . you're . . ."

Benedict Blackwood laughed loudly, slapping his fat belly with glee.

"I'm what, pipsqueak?" he asked through his laughter. "You're going to call me a mean name? Go ahead. You really think you can hurt my feelings? I'm the dastardliest criminal in the world! People tremble with fear at the very sound of my name! I'm the most terrifying human being on the planet. I once said 'boo' to a man and his knees fell off! There's nothing you can say that can hurt me. Go ahead, pipsqueak. Do your best. What am I?"

"You're a fustilarian, sock stinkin', ear hair pluckin', chipmunk kissin', cream-faced genuphobe goon to the twelfth power!"

I had no idea what most of those words meant, but I remembered seeing some of them in a book in my parents' garage. And some of them I might have made up. But even though I didn't understand what I said, I meant every word of it.

All of the criminals took in deep breaths as their eyes darted over to their king. Rose Blackwood stared at me in disbelief. My parents crossed their eyes, confused by my string of long and confusing words.

Benedict Blackwood's mean and rotten face stared at me blankly, and then I saw something that I never expected to see.

Two, big, fat tears poured from the villain's eyes, followed by two more, and two more, and two more.

"Your Highness? Are . . . are you crying?" one of the criminals asked.

"No!" Benedict Blackwood shouted as he furiously

wiped at his eyes. "I just have something in my eyes! Everybody stop looking at me. Now! I order you not to look at me! And I'm not crying! I think some rain just landed on my face!" He let out a sudden sob.

Everyone looked away from the crying king and pretended to pick their nails, scratch their toes, or fix their hair. Those of us who had our hands tied just looked around and whistled.

When the king finally stopped crying, he told us that we could look at him again.

"You'll all be going to jail for the rest of your pitiful lives," he told us. He blew his nose on one of his criminal associate's sleeves before he turned towards me. "Except for you, pipsqueak. You won't be going there. I have special plans for you."

In just one week, I had angered the most dangerous man in the world, and I had knocked out the one man alive who could save me from him.

Yup, it's been a busy week for good old W.B.

"Pipsqueak! Go stand against that wall!" Benedict Blackwood roared as he pointed to a large wall across the street.

I looked at my parents, who looked absolutely terrified.

"Just do what he says, my son," said P in a shaky voice.

"Yes, just do what he says," M whispered with tears in her eyes.

Rose pleaded with her brother, but no one could understand her through the gag tied around her mouth.

I crossed the street and stood against the wall, facing Benedict Blackwood.

The King of Arizona Territory reached over his shoulder and produced a crossbow. The rain began to fall harder. He took an arrow and strung the bow. My parents both cried out. Rose Blackwood fainted.

The strange thing was I didn't feel afraid. When I thought about everything I'd already been through and all of the challenges I'd faced, how I'd hung out of windows hundreds of feet in the air, run from mad inventors, dodged bullets, and avoided wild pigs . . . this just didn't seem that scary to me. I had grown brave, braver than I ever thought I could be. I was so calm that I actually yawned. This man was clearly just trying to frighten me.

And then one of the criminals put a little kidney bean on top of my head.

"What's that for?" I asked.

Benedict Blackwood grinned, showing his mouthful of yellowing teeth. "Target practice," he said. "I'm going to shoot the bean off the top of your head."

"But . . . but that arrowhead is much larger than the bean. If you hit the bean, you're probably going to hit my head too. And if that arrow hits my head, it's goodbye W.B.," I told him.

"I know."

!!!!

Nope. Forget what I said earlier. I take back what I said about braveness. I was afraid. I was very afraid. I was just a coward, perhaps the most cowardly coward who has ever cowed. I was a yellow-bellied chicken who also has a yellow streak down his back, down his front, and running down the inside of his leg.

Benedict aimed his crossbow at my head, started to pull the trigger, and then, just before his very sharp looking arrow could find a new home in the middle of my fore-head. . . I suddenly felt something powerful grab me.

I gasped, and then realized that I was moving. In fact, I was moving quite quickly, galloping across the town of Pitchfork at a breakneck pace.

"Climb up, Wide Butt!" a familiar voice cried. "You're too heavy for me to hold for much longer!"

I looked up and saw a face that I had missed very much.

Magnus, our horse. Magnus grunted his hello, and then turned to face forward so he could continue galloping us to safety.

I looked up even higher and saw another face that I had missed.

"You're pretty clever giving me that clue in your address. By the way, I found the horse thief who stole Magnus. The horse thief traded him to me in exchange for one of my fists to his nose. Come on, W.B., up you go!" Shorty said with a grin.

I crawled up onto the saddle behind Shorty, and she helped undo the ropes tying my wrists together.

"Thanks, Shorty. But how are we going to save my family? Benedict Blackwood still has them."

"I don't know," she answered. "You're the brains here. I'm just the muscle. If you're really expecting to defeat Benedict Blackwood, you're going to need an awfully brilliant plan. I heard he's so mean that his own shadow won't hang out with him."

Drat. I was hoping I wouldn't have to come up with a brilliant plan. I'm much better at silly ideas and idiotic suggestions. I wished my parents could help. They were the brilliant ones. They could probably use their knowledge of science to hatch a great plan for defeating Benedict Blackwood.

As we continued to ride, I could see the storm clouds moving quickly overhead. The rain was falling even harder now, and then I heard the first rumbling of thunder.

"You might want to think of a plan fast," Shorty said through her chattering teeth. "I'm getting wetter than a toothless man bobbing for apples in a lopsided pig trough."

I tried my best to think of a plan. My poor parents and Rose were being taken to jail by Benedict Blackwood and his criminal gang. But what could I do to save them? I was only one kid; I only had one other kid and a horse to help me. The criminals would have no trouble stopping us if we tried to break into the jail to free my parents. There were so many of them. It would take an army to defeat all of those criminals. I needed to come up with a plan, and I needed to come up with it fast. *Fast . . . fast?*

Fast! That's it!

I've got it! I think! Maybe?

No?

Wait . . . do I?

Yes! I have it!

"Shorty!" I cried in excitement. "I have a plan! Magnus! I need you to start running as fast as you can in that direction, and when I tell you to stop, then stop! Okay?"

Both Magnus and Shorty looked at me as though I was nutty, but then they shrugged their shoulders.

"Alright," said Shorty. She dug her heel into Magnus's side and shook his reins. "I hope you know what you're doing, W.B."

I hoped so too.

Magnus began to charge, running as fast as he possibly could. He was helped by the electric horseshoes that my father had invented for him—they actually doubled his speed, making him the fastest horse alive. Magnus ran so fast that Shorty's hat whipped off her head, and my handkerchief flew off my neck. He ran so fast that the winds almost ripped us from his saddle. Magnus galloped through rock and muck, his hooves echoing the thunder overhead.

"Faster!" I screamed. "Run faster, Magnus! Go as fast as you can, and then go twice as fast as that!"

I could tell I was annoying my horse with my screams, but he still obeyed me. It wasn't often that Magnus was given the chance to run as fast as he could—he was usually forced to trot slowly when my parents rode him into town. But this was his chance to show just how fast he could go. He ran all the way out of Pitchfork and deep into the desert, where the sandy hills were turning muddy from the rain.

Soon he was moving so fast that the entire desert

looked like a blur. Shorty tried to YEE-HAW in excitement, but we were galloping faster than the speed of sound, so her YEE-HAW couldn't be heard until thirty seconds after she'd already said it.

Finally, when I decided that we had gone far and fast enough, I leaned forward and shouted into Magnus's ears.

"STOP!!"

The horse came to an immediate stop, his electric horse shoes causing sparks to fly across the rocky ground as he skidded.

I shouted over the pounding of the rain, "Now turn around and start running as fast as you can in the other direction!"

Magnus was too excited by his amazing run to question why I'd want him to do that. He immediately spun around and began to run, galloping as quickly as he could. His legs churned like the pistons on one of my parents' weird inventions. He was moving so fast that it seemed as though he was about to take flight. He looked like a grey streak of lightning tearing across the desert.

"Magnus, look out!" screamed Shorty.

"Magnus, look out!" screamed Shorty.

"Magnus, look out!" screamed Shorty.

There were more and more screams as Magnus, Shorty,

and I all crashed into the previous versions of ourselves, the ones who existed in a slightly earlier time.

Are you confused?

Allow me to explain.

Magnus, Shorty and I had traveled into the east so quickly, then turned around and traveled into the west so quickly that we had *gone ahead in time,* then turned around and went *back* in time and crashed into an earlier version of ourselves who were still running into the future.

And the earlier version of Magnus, Shorty, and I had also traveled so quickly from the east to the west that they had crashed into earlier versions of *themselves* as well. And *they* had crashed into earlier versions of *themselves.* And so on, and so on, and so on. There was roughly one hundred of each of us lining the path in a crumpled heap from our terrible crashes.

Yes! It worked! It actually worked! I thought.

I told my parents that it was possible! They said it couldn't be done! But I proved them wrong! I proved them all wrong! A hah! Ahahaha! Bahaha! Ahahah—ahem.

Excuse me. Sorry about that.

I now understand why my father does that. Sometimes laughing maniacally feels really good.

Though I was thrown from the saddle and was upside

down in a muddy sand dune, I had a big smile on my face.

I now had my army. All of the earlier versions of me, Shorty, and Magnus were together.

"Golly," said Shorty as she looked at the earlier versions of herself.

"Golly," said Shorty as she looked at the earlier versions of herself.

"Golly," said Shorty as she looked at the earlier versions of herself.

"You can say that again," I said.

"You can say that again," I said.

"You can say that again," I said.

"Nayyyyy?" said Magnus.

"Nayyyyy?" said Magnus.

"Nayyyyy?" said Magnus.

While every Shorty stared in disbelief at every W.B., every Magnus looked around and exhaled in confusion, a hundred horses snorting all at once.

COOKED HIS FEET IN HIS BOOTS

I quickly learned that there was a problem with having an army of yourself. For one thing, everyone wanted to be in charge. Especially all of the W.B.s.

"Alright!" I called out to everyone. "This is what we're going to do!"

"Okay!" another W.B. called out. "This is the plan!"

"Listen up!" another one yelled. "This is what will happen!"

"Naaayyyy!" said Magnus.

"Nayyyyyy!" said another Magnus.

"Be quiet!" bellowed my Shorty. "Listen to my W.B.! He's the one who came up with this plan!"

"No, he didn't!" another Shorty yelled back. "My W.B. came up with the plan! Your W.B. just followed it!"

"How could he?" my Shorty challenged. "My W.B. is the oldest W.B., which means he came up with the plan first! He's in charge! And if anyone disagrees with me, you can come on over here and watch me bop you on the nose!"

After that everyone else was quiet. All of the Shortys knew that Shorty never made threats like that unless she meant them, and all of the W.B.s were secretly afraid of her. And none of the Magnuses really cared.

"Alright," I said, "here is our plan . . ."

And it was a good one.

There were over fifty criminals standing guard at the Pitchfork jailhouse. They all hated the job. For one thing, most of them had spent their lives trying to escape jail, and now they were being forced to guard one.

"It don't make no sense, does it?" one criminal asked another.

"That's a double negative," the other criminal answered. "If you say *it don't make no sense*, what you're actually saying is *it does make sense*. I think what you want to say is that it doesn't—"

But before he could finish telling the other criminal

what he should have said, he found that his mouth was suddenly interrupted by a very dirty and hairy fist. The two criminals began to fight one another, which frequently happened when one of them would attempt to correct another's grammar. Criminals are very sensitive about their grammar.

And then one of them spotted us.

"Hey!" cried the criminal guard. "Stop fighting, fellas! Look! It's the kid! And he's got a friend!"

"And a horse! Let's get him!" another criminal shouted.

"One at a time," one of the taller criminal guards warned. "King Benedict said that we can't all leave the jail at the same time. Only one of us can go."

"How do we decide who gets to go after the kid?" a criminal asked.

"We could draw straws?" one suggested.

But they didn't have straws.

"We could flip a coin?" another suggested.

But Benedict Blackwood had taken all of their coins.

"We could go by whoever has the smelliest socks?" a third criminal suggested.

Two minutes later, a criminal by the name of Sheepy Joe was selected as the winner of the smelliest socks contest. Sheepy Joe hopped onto his horse and galloped over towards the two kids on their horse.

"Try and catch me!" shouted W.B.

"That's what I was going to do!" Sheepy Joe grunted.

The rain was now coming down in huge sheets of water, and as Sheepy Joe and his horse splashed through puddles and mud, the kids and their horse galloped several paces ahead of him.

After a quick ride through the town, Sheepy Joe finally trapped the kids and their horse in an alleyway.

"I've got you now!" he cackled. "Benedict Blackwood will be so glad that I caught you, he might even buy me a new pair of socks!"

"You didn't catch us, though," said Shorty. "In fact, we're getting away."

"Huh?" said Sheepy Joe, his frown falling somewhere into his scraggly beard.

"It's true. Look behind you. We're already running out of town," said W.B.

Sheepy Joe turned his head in time to see W.B., Shorty, and Magnus riding away in the other direction.

"Dagnabbit," Sheepy Joe muttered to himself as he spun his horse around and began to follow them out of town. "I'll get you kids!"

The W.B., Shorty, and Magnus in the alleyway smiled.

One down, fifty-five to go.

The later versions of Shorty, Magnus, and W.B. lured all of the criminal guards away from the jail and out of town, allowing me, Shorty, and Magnus the chance to stroll right into the jail and free my parents and the deputies.

It was almost too easy.

I tried to stroll inside, but I stumbled on my boot and fell face forward into a mud pit. Luckily, I had some experience falling face forward into mud pits, so I knew the best way to do it.

"Wow," said Shorty. "I've never seen someone fall into a mud pit so gracefully."

I cleared the mud from my left ear and opened the door to the jailhouse.

The deputies from Chicago were all locked up in one cell, while my parents and Rose Blackwood were locked up in another. Everyone was bundled together and shivering with their eyes squeezed tightly shut. The tin roof of the jailhouse leaked, and there were large puddles of water on the floor. It was freezing inside. The only thing heating the room was a single candle.

I whispered, "Hey everybody?"

"Shhhh. Can't you see we're trying to sleep, kid?" one of the deputies said.

My parents both opened their eyes and rushed to the door of their jail cell.

"W.B.!" my father gasped.

"How did you get in here?" M asked. "There were over fifty guards outside!"

I smiled brightly and told my parents about my brilliant plan, how I had used science to lure each and every one of the criminal guards away so that they would be stuck chasing earlier versions of me. My parents stood there and listened to me explain, and the longer that I explained, the longer their frowns became. Finally, I finished explaining and waited for them to shower me with compliments.

"That's the stupidest thing I've ever heard," said P. "You can't form an army out of earlier versions of you, because time travel is not possible. And it certainly isn't possible by running really fast on a horse. Oh, hi Magnus."

Magnus snorted a hello.

"Your story makes no sense," M added as she scratched her head. "You really weren't listening when I was explaining time zones to you, were you?"

I rolled my eyes.

"I listened to part of it, but your explanations are always so long. I got bored while you were talking and sort of started zoning out and thinking about other things," I told her.

"You were thinking about squirrels, weren't you?" Rose said with a half-smile on her face.

"Maybe."

"Well," my mother said, "if you had listened the whole time you would know that what you just did is impossible. You cannot travel in time and join forces with earlier versions of yourself. It's impossible."

"Totally impossible. And not only is it impossible, it's also very silly." P continued.

"Alright," I snapped, annoyed that they weren't proud of me for what I'd done. "I rescued you in a totally impossible and very silly way. Okay? Are you happy now?"

"Yes," my mother said with a grin. "Thank you, W.B. The keys to our cells are on that table over there. Would you mind letting us out so we can escape?"

I unlocked the cell holding my

parents and Rose Blackwood, and Shorty unlocked the cell holding all of the deputies.

One of the deputies halted as he was stepping out of the cell. "Wait. Is Benedict Blackwood still out there somewhere?"

"Yes, he is," Rose told him. "But we're going to capture him. I owe it to everyone to make sure he's put behind bars for the rest of his life."

"Oh. In that case, we'll just stay here. Please close the door behind you. Thank you."

Shorty closed the deputies' cell door quietly and allowed them to go back to sleep.

We all stepped out of the jailhouse with Rose Blackwood leading the way. The rain had gone from falling droplets to falling in sheets, to falling as though someone was pouring a bucket of ice water over our heads. The thunder was rumbling louder, and, for the first time, I saw flashes of lightning against the darkened sky.

The winds and rains were now so strong that the streets were completely empty. The fires in the buildings had all gone out.

"Where are we going?" I asked Rose.

A loud crack of thunder echoed against the clouds, and we were all forced to cover our ears. Rose Blackwood pointed up ahead to a large clock tower located in the center of town.

"I heard one of the criminals from the jail say that Benedict has been living in the clock tower!" Rose shouted over the sound of the storm. "We need to go there and challenge him to a duel! Otherwise, he'll start taking over cities all over the country! I know my brother! He'll grow so strong that no one will ever be able to stop him!"

"Oh dear," said my father.

"I don't think I want to live in a world where that horrible man is in charge," M said.

"Then we'll have to fight him. We have to do what Sheriff Hoyt Graham would do. Come on!" I told them.

I had read about that clock tower in my Sheriff Hoyt Graham books. On the dirt road in front of the clock tower is where the sheriff had all of his duels with the villains who committed crimes in his town. They would stand in front of the clock tower and face one another, the clock would strike noon, and then they would draw their guns and fire. The winner was the one who wasn't dead.

According to his books, Sheriff Hoyt Graham had

won over five hundred of those duels. Benedict Blackwood had won over seven hundred. M, P, Rose, and I had won roughly none. But if what Benedict Blackwood wanted was a duel, then that's what was going to happen. He wasn't the sort of fellow who would allow you to suggest a game of tiddlywinks or a tickle fight instead.

By the time we reached the open area in front of the clock tower, we had spotted Benedict Blackwood. He was seated beneath an awning, polishing his crown. Two members of his criminal gang were sitting with him. Actually, Benedict was sitting on one of them and using the other one as a footstool.

"Hello, Ben!" Rose Blackwood shouted.

Benedict Blackwood stopped polishing his crown and looked up at his sister. He smiled an awful smile.

"That's King Ben to you, commoner," he called back. "How did you escape from jail? I would have never guessed that a goody two shoes like you would be able to manage something like that!"

"Goody two shoes? What does that mean? What's wrong with having two shoes? How many is a person supposed to have?" my father asked with a confused expression on his face.

"I had a bit of help," Rose told her brother. "And now

I've come to send you back to jail for good. I challenge you to a duel!"

Benedict Blackwood laughed long and hard at that. The criminal he was using as a footstool laughed too. The criminal he was using as a chair tried to laugh, but he couldn't because he had all of Benedict's weight on his back.

"You want to challenge me? That's the funniest thing I've ever heard! Have you even fired a gun before?" he sneered.

"Yes," Rose said defensively. "Once."

"It's true! She didn't hit anyone, but she scared off a bunch of wild pigs. Scary wild pigs!" I said.

"That's not really helping," Rose whispered to me.

A streak of lightning cut across the black storm clouds as Benedict Blackwood stood up and slowly strutted over to us. I noticed two very large revolvers strapped to his sides, as well as six knives buckled to his boots, a bow and arrow over his shoulder, a crossbow on his back, a sword sheathed on his thigh, a lasso around his waist, a slingshot in his back pocket, a tomahawk in his long underwear, and I could tell from the way that his shirt bulged with random pointy bits that he had even more weapons hidden on him. He was also a darn good shot, which meant he would be almost impossible to defeat in a duel. He was practically a walking weapon.

"Alright," said Benedict Blackwood, "I accept your challenge. In fact, I challenge *all* of you. You'll all duel me, one on one. The winner gets to rule the town."

"What about the loser?" P asked.

"The loser gets to be dead."

"Oh."

"Well, let's get started!" Benedict cried, rubbing his hands together in excitement. "I can't wait to hurt you all very badly. I'm really looking forward to it. Thank you for escaping from jail. This has really made my day."

I raised my hand.

Benedict Blackwood pointed to me.

"Yes? The boy with his hair parted on the wrong side."

"Quick question," I said. "How did Sheriff Hoyt Graham defeat you in a duel last time?"

Benedict rolled his eyes.

"Oh, that goody-goody insisted that we fight without using weapons. He beat me in a fistfight when he knocked me unconscious. I didn't even see the old man's punch coming. Alright, which one of you wants to go first?"

"I insist that we fight without weapons!" I cried out.

Benedict Blackwood frowned for a moment, but then his mouth turned up in a devious smile when he realized he'd get the chance to pummel my face with his bare hands.

"Alright, pipsqueak," he said as he cracked his knuckles. "I'll beat you all in a fist fight. One at a time. Who's first?"

"That was quite clever, W.B.," M said to me. "Finding out how this man had been beaten in the past. Your brain is starting to think like a scientist's."

"Yes, it was very clever," P said as he patted my head. "I'm very proud of you, son."

I smiled.

"You there! You with the funny white hair! You're first. Come here and let me pound you into chicken feed." Benedict Blackwood shouted, pointing at my father.

"Alright," my father said as he made his way over to the King of Arizona Territory, "but first I should explain to you that that's not actually how chicken feed is made. You see, chicken feed is a nutritious grain, and it is made by—"

Benedict Blackwood wasn't interested in hearing about how chicken feed was made. Well, he might have been interested, but not at that moment. At that moment he was interested in beating P to bits. He jumped on my father and tried to twist his head off.

"I don't think heads can actually twist off!" P choked as he tried to fight back.

"Well, I'm performing an experiment to find out for

sure!" Benedict shouted as he continued to twist.

My father yelped in pain.

"McLaron!" my mother cried.

"Mr. Baron!" Rose cried.

"P!" I cried.

"Wide Butt's dad!" Shorty cried.

"Nayyy!" Magnus cried.

My father managed to wriggle away from Benedict Blackwood's strong grip, but the criminal king was too fast and too strong to be wriggled away from for too long. He grabbed my father by the back of the head and began to mash his face in the mud. The storm clouds were now so dark and the rain was so thick that we could barely see them fighting. But I could hear my father gargle as he tried to pull his face out of the muddy water. I wished I could go help him, but if we broke the rules and tried to gang up on Benedict Blackwood, there was a good chance Benedict Blackwood would break the rules and use one of his many weapons. And then we wouldn't stand a chance.

"McLaron!" M shouted again.

"I'm sort of busy right now, Sharon," P called back, as Benedict forced him to punch himself in the eye with his own fist.

"Why are you hitting yourself?" Benedict cackled

madly.

"Because you're making me!"

"McLaron!" my mother cried at the top of her lungs.

"He's in the middle of something right now," Benedict Blackwood yelled, "but if you leave me a message, I'll be certain that he gets back to you later."

"McLaron!!" my mother bellowed in a voice so loud it actually made the thunder hush.

My father and Benedict stopped fighting. For a moment there was no sound except for the patter of the rain.

"Yes, my little muffin?" P said.

"Use science."

Suddenly, Aunt Dorcas appeared at the other end of the street. She looked at us and shrieked.

"Oh, for the love of . . . who let her out?" Benedict Blackwood asked us angrily.

"Not me."

"Me neither."

"I prefer to keep her locked away."

"I don't know who that is."

"Nayyyyyy!"

"What do you mean, *use science*?" P asked M, looking quite confused. "I should use science to defeat Benedict

Blackwood?"

My mother smiled at him while slowly pointing to her head.

"Yes," she said. "Use science, McLaron. *Use your head.*"

Aunt Dorcas spotted Benedict Blackwood and shrieked again, fainting into a mud puddle. I started to walk across the street to help her, but then I changed my mind. I'd help her later. Maybe.

My father suddenly got the look in his eye that he did when my mother showed him how to fix a problem with one of his inventions.

"Use . . . my head. Alright, my little muffin."

P hopped up from the mud puddle and quickly climbed onto Benedict Blackwood's large back.

"Huh? What are you doing?" Benedict questioned as he tried to swat at him.

But P avoided his large hands. Soon he had crawled on top of his shoulders and wrapped his arms and legs around Benedict's neck. He pointed his head high into the air and smiled.

"Are you trying to choke me?" Benedict asked. "You're not wrapping your arms or legs tight enough around my neck to choke me. My neck is too strong for you to choke me anyway. You're failing, you white haired fool. All I need to do is throw you off me, stomp on your head, and I'll be ready to move on to the next challenger. I think I'll fight your chubby little son next. I'm really going to enjoy crushing his head until it looks like—"

Suddenly we were all blinded by a large flash of lightning which exploded in front of the clock tower.

I told you before that my father's head attracts lightning the way that picnics attract ants. He's been struck by lightning so many times that it doesn't really bother him anymore.

But Benedict Blackwood wasn't as used to lightning strikes as my father was. Most people aren't. The lightning bolt that hit him and my father knocked King Benedict Blackwood unconscious and cooked his feet in his boots.

Even Better Than
a Strange Dream

My dream of having my hero pin a medal on me finally came true. Once we released the deputies from jail and all of Sheriff Graham's other deputies came back to town, they were able to clean up the mess that Benedict Blackwood had made. The rest of the criminals were jailed. The garbage was cleaned up. The bank vaults were filled with money again. And the restaurants and shops that Benedict Blackwood had made into outhouses . . . well, they got rid of those.

My father had to go to the hospital to make sure he was alright after the lightning strike, and he was, although his hair was a bit whiter and pointier than it was before. Benedict Blackwood was alright too, though his feet now resembled a pair of freshly barbecued sausages.

It was in that hospital that I was finally introduced to Sheriff Hoyt Graham. He was in bed recovering from being hit in the head by the fountain pen.

The sheriff was a lot older than I thought he would be. And he was a lot smaller too. I pictured him as the strong and handsome young man on the cover of all his novels, but instead he was thin and pale, skinny and frail, with more hair in his ears than on top of his head.

"Are you the kid who helped bring down Benedict Blackwood?" he asked when he saw me.

"Yes, sir, Sheriff Graham, sir," I said with a bow. "It's an honor to meet you. I've read all of your books."

"Oh, you have?" he asked with a smile. "Well, isn't that nice. I plan on reading all of them too, once I finally learn how to read."

I frowned.

"You mean . . . you didn't write them?" I asked.

The sheriff suddenly made a horrible wheezing sound. I was about to run out of the room to find a doctor or nurse to help him when suddenly I realized that the horrible wheezing sound was laughter.

"Of course I didn't write them," the sheriff said. He took a large swig from the water glass on his bedside table before continuing, "I never went to school. In fact, I can't read anything other than my name. And not even my full name, just my middle name. Opie. It's written over there on that door. See?"

I looked over to the door he was pointing at. It said "OPEN." I decided not to correct the sheriff on the only word he thought he could read. It didn't seem right to correct a man as great as him.

"Well, even if you didn't write them, you've still lived through all sorts of fantastic adventures," I said. "Like the time you saved Pitchfork from fifty invaders."

"Well . . ." Sheriff Graham said slowly, "that's not exactly true. In fact, I've been told that the fellow who writes my books will occasionally stretch the truth about my heroic adventures. Just a bit."

"Stretch the truth? What do you mean?" I asked.

"I mean," he began, "I didn't *actually* save the town from fifty invaders. I saved the town from five—"

"Five invaders?" I said, barely able to hide my disappointment. "Well, I suppose that's not too bad. It still must be difficult to fight off five invaders."

"Oh, I'm sure it is," the sheriff agreed. "Only I didn't fight off five invaders. I fought off five skunks."

"Skunks?"

"But they were mean skunks!" Sheriff Graham insisted. "Sprayed me at least a half dozen times. I smelled like the underside of a mule for a good three weeks after that. But I fought them all off. And they've never been back to Pitchfork. Except maybe once or twice. Maybe three times. Maybe they're still living here. Under my house. But the important thing is I tried. The truth is I'm not much of a fighter. Never have been."

"Then how did you defeat Benedict Blackwood in a fistfight?" I asked, unable to believe my ears.

"A piece of the clock tower broke off and landed on his head," Sheriff Graham said with a chuckle. "It knocked him unconscious. If that hadn't happened, he would have punched me into next week. I couldn't win a fistfight if my opponent was blindfolded with both hands tied behind his back, and his feet were slathered in bacon grease."

"Are all of your stories lies?" I asked quietly.

"No! Absolutely not. No. Not a bit. Well, sort of. A couple are lies. Some of them are lies, I mean. Most of them. Most of them are lies. Quite a lot of them, in fact. About ninety-nine point nine percent are lies. Alright, all of them are lies."

I stared at the little old man in disbelief. I'd been reading those fantastic stories about him for so long. He'd been my personal hero, the man who I looked up to more than anyone else. But he was nothing more than a fraud, a fake, a lie created by a writer in order to sell books. At that moment I wanted nothing more than to run out of that hospital room and never look back.

The sheriff sensed that I was upset. "Wait. I want you to know, kid, that even though I'm not your hero anymore, you're definitely one of mine. What you and your family did is incredible. My doctor told me about your parents, and how they actually managed to build a floating house."

"A flying house," I corrected.

"A *flying* house? Wow!" Sheriff Graham exclaimed. "That's even more impressive. Boy, I bet your parents are the smartest people who ever lived. I wish my parents were like that. Then maybe I would have learned to read and learned about science and stuff like that. You must be really, really proud of them."

And he was right.

"I am," I told Sheriff Graham. "And thank you, Sheriff Graham. Even if your stories aren't true, I sure did enjoy reading them. I hope you'll be out of here soon so you can go back to work protecting Pitchfork from invaders, or skunks, or whatever."

The sheriff smiled a gummy smile, and then he suddenly remembered something.

"Oooh, wait!" he said, as he reached under his pillow. "I got something for you, kid. It's a medal. All heroes deserve a medal. Normally, my deputies pick out the medals I give to people, since I can't read what's written on them. But I chose this one myself. I want you to have it, kid. You deserve it."

He pulled out a brass medal and held it up to me. I smiled proudly. It no longer mattered to me that Sheriff Graham wasn't the man he was in his books. I was still happy to get a medal from him.

I leaned forward, and he pinned it to the front of my shirt. I lifted it and read the inscription: "WORLD'S GREATEST GRANDMA."

My mother and father were eventually able to repair the Baron Estate, and, once we had gathered enough coal for the trip, we were up and running.

Shorty had to go back to Chicago, so we flew her home right away. Her father and her mother were terribly worried about her. She hadn't told them that she was coming out to Pitchfork with Magnus to save me.

My father ended up giving Magnus to Shorty as a thank you gift. Shorty was excited about that, but Magnus was even more excited. Living with Shorty meant he would be treated like a normal horse, which meant he wouldn't have to wear any of my father's strange new inventions anymore. Shorty made me promise to write to her every day. When I told her I would try, she grabbed me by my nose and twisted it until I promised that I would *definitely* write to her every day.

The deputies in Pitchfork decided not to send Rose Blackwood to jail for kidnapping us, since she helped us capture her brother, and because my parents convinced them that she was really a good person.

When my parents asked Rose where we should drop

her off, she broke into tears.

"I don't know," she confessed. "I can't go back to my parents' house in Chicago. They'll be furious that Benedict is back in jail. They told me not to come back until I'd freed him. When they hear that I helped put him back into jail, they'll never want to speak to me again. I guess it doesn't really matter where you leave me. I have no home."

It did sound like an awful problem. After my mother and father left the room to have a private talk with each other, they came back and offered Rose Blackwood an unexpected deal.

"We'd like to invite you to stay with us, Rose," M told her. "But there are some things that we will expect of you. You will have to help us with our science projects. You can act as our assistant. We can't afford to pay you yet, but we'll give you a room to sleep in and three fresh meals a day."

Suddenly it all made sense to me. This was why they had treated Rose so kindly after she had kidnapped us and why my father had let her fly the Baron Estate back to Chicago. M and P must have seen something in Rose Blackwood from the start, something clever and kind, which they appreciated. I bet my parents, who I honestly believe are the smartest people in the world, knew that Rose Blackwood would one day become their assistant.

They probably knew it from the moment they laid eyes on her.

M saw me staring at her and winked.

Rose Blackwood smiled so widely that I was able to count each one of her brightly shining teeth.

"Of course!" she cried. "That sounds wonderful! In fact, it sounds like a dream come true!"

"You'll also have to help watch over W.B.," P said.

"Yes!" Rose said, grabbing me and pulling me in for a big hug. "I would love that! W.B. is like a little brother to me! In fact, he's better than a brother! I actually *like* him!"

"And finally, you'll also have to help with Aunt Dorcas," M concluded.

The smile ran away from Rose's face. For a moment she looked as though she might throw up, but then she quickly pulled herself together.

"Alright," she finally said. "I guess there had to be a catch. Oh well. It's a deal."

Home. After travelling around the entire country we were home. I used to think we lived in the most boring place in the world, but once we landed the flying Baron

Estate back on our property in Arizona Territory, near the little creek where we would wade and fish, next to the fields where we picked dandelions and had picnics, by our shed and our mailbox, and the little white fence that ran along our land, I realized that I had been absolutely right. It was the most boring place in the world. But it was still ours.

While I still read my Sheriff Hoyt Graham books, I've started reading my parents' science and mathematics books as well. They're not as interesting. In fact, sometimes they're so boring that I literally fall asleep in the middle of a sentence. But they're the sort of books that my heroes M and P enjoy, so I want to try my best to understand them. After all, they've recently started trying to understand me; which is impressive, since *I* don't even really understand me.

It was early afternoon. School was out for the summer. I was sitting on the sofa in the living room, trying to read a book that M had given me about winged flying machines, when suddenly I heard a familiar pounding down the hall-way.

Oh no.

"Helloooo!" a horrible voice sang. "Hellooooo little Waldo!"

Oh no.

I closed my eyes and pretended to be asleep.

"I knooow you're just pretennnnding to be asleeeeep!" Aunt Dorcas sang.

My eyes popped open.

"Yes, I was faking it," I said. "What do you want, Aunt Dorcas? And do you really have to sing so much?"

"Yes I dooooooooooooooooo! I doooooo beeee doooo beee doooooo!" she sang.

I buried my head under a pillow until she stopped singing.

When it was safe, I poked my head back out.

"Are you finished?" I asked.

"For now, yes," she said with a wide smile. "Do you know what today is?"

I did. It was my eleventh birthday.

"It's my birthday. And, as a birthday gift, I'd like for you not to sing to me anymore," I told her.

"Deal," said Aunt Dorcas, and then she held up a large bag. "This is a gift from Rose and your parents. Happy birthday, Waldo."

She set the bag on the table in front of me and gave me a kiss on top of my head before leaving.

I stared at the bag with a funny feeling in my stomach. Was I asleep? Was this a dream? Was I going to open the bag and find myself staring at squirrel versions of my parents? Did I eat fry bread with hard cheese and baked beans with hot chilies again last night?

Moving very slowly, I leaned forward and reached into the bag, expecting to feel a cage with a talking squirrel in it. Instead, I felt something made of wood, metal, and canvas. I pulled the item out of the bag and was delighted by what I saw.

It was a toy flying machine. It looked like a little version of the flying machines from the book that I was reading. It was absolutely beautiful, with a sleek, wooden body, and wide, canvas wings. There were four deep compartments where the riders would sit, and a pair of wheels at the bottom for landings. There was a metal propeller at the front of each wing, as well as on the nose and on the tail, and, when I flicked them with my finger, they spun around and around. I had never seen a toy like this in a shop, and I knew right away that my parents had made it for me.

It was the greatest gift that anyone had ever given me. I picked it up and immediately pretended to fly it through the living room.

As I jumped up and swung my flying machine through the air, I heard a little voice say, "Careful, W.B.!"

I stopped and looked around.

"Hello?" I said, looking down the hall. "Who said that?"

"I did!"

I looked down at the flying machine.

Suddenly, three small heads popped out from the seating compartments in the toy glider. It was M, P, and Rose. Somehow, they had shrunk themselves to fit in my new toy glider.

For a moment I didn't believe what I was seeing. I set the glider down on the table and rubbed my eyes. I looked again, and they were still there. I rubbed my eyes again and then pinched myself.

"Try bonking yourself on the head with that book," little Rose suggested. "That'll prove that you're awake, and we've really shrunk ourselves."

I took the book on flying machines and whacked myself over the head with it.

"Ow."

"See?" said little Rose with a giggle. "You're awake."

"This is all thanks to you, W.B. Your silly dream about talking squirrels inspired me to invent something new, a machine that will shrink you to the size of a squirrel!" said my tiny father.

"Is it permanent? Are you going to be that tiny forever?" I asked.

"No," said my tiny mother. "It will last as long as we want it to. You see, we thought it might be fun to fly around the country again. But the flying Baron Estate was so large, that it attracted a lot of attention and required a lot of coal to power it. We figured if we fly around in a mini flying machine, no one will notice us, and we'll have a chance to really see the world."

"Not only that," P continued, his tiny grin growing wider. "But I also built a tiny underwater ship which will allow us to explore the deepest parts of the sea, and a tiny rocket which will allow us to fly all the way into outer space! It's much easier to build tiny versions of these things. They don't require as much material, and I can keep them all in my closet. I don't know why I didn't invent tiny versions of things and a shrinking machine sooner. It's so convenient."

"Oh," I said, suddenly feeling disappointed. "So this little flying machine isn't really my birthday gift."

"That's where you're wrong, W.B.," said tiny Rose Blackwood with a wink. "This flying machine is one hundred percent yours. You are the captain. We are your crew. And we will go anywhere in the world that you'd like to go."

"All you need to do is allow yourself to be shrunk, and we can get started. Do you mind if I shrink you, son?" asked tiny P as he held up a little mechanical box.

What's a kid expected to say to something like that?

"Go ahead," I said with a smile. "Shrink away."

He pressed a little button in the center of the box, and, the next thing I knew, everything was giant except for me.

I had been shrunk.

I climbed into the front seat of the flying machine and marveled at all the fancy controls. Now that I was tiny, I could see just how much detail my father had put into the flying machine. It was incredible.

"May I please be the first mate, Captain W.B.?" P asked.

"Sure. But I don't have a nifty cap for you to wear."

P reached into his pocket and pulled out a tiny cap that said "FIRST MATE" on it. "That's alright," he told me. "I brought my own."

"Where would you like to go, W.B.?" M asked, squeezing my shoulders excitedly as she buckled me into my seat. "You can go anywhere in the world."

"Aunt Dorcas is watching the house for us. She said her birthday gift to you is not coming along on our trip," Rose added.

"That's very kind of her," I said.

"She really is a good egg, isn't she?" said P.

"So where are we going, Captain?" M asked. "Egypt? Italy? Ireland? France? We'll go anywhere that your heart desires."

"Anywhere at all, little brother," Rose echoed as she tousled my hair.

"I'd like to see everything and everywhere," I told them.

My family laughed and cheered.

"Alright," P said. "But where should we go first?"

I thought for a moment.

"First," I told him, "I'd like to fly to the highest point of the Rocky Mountains."

"Aye aye, Captain!" my parents cried as they started the little flying machine.

We began to roll across the little coffee table and then the propellers began to spin. The next thing I knew, we were flying. We did flips and loops and spins all throughout the living room, and then zipped into the hallway and down to the kitchen where Aunt Dorcas was waiting by the back door. She was eating a hardboiled egg as she opened the back door to let us out with a wave and a cheery farewell.

Our little flying machine flew with the grace of a bird, sailing high into the endless blue of the Arizona Territory sky in search of the Rocky Mountains. As we flew, we came upon a collection of ducks flying in a V-shaped pattern. Rose and I waved to them. They looked at us, and, though ducks don't have lips, I could swear that they were smiling.

Sometimes life is even better than a strange dream.

ALL HAIL THE FURRY EMPRESS

Eric Bower and his lovely wife, Laura, live in utter terror of their cat, who rules their small cottage in Pasadena, California with an iron paw. Eric can't quite recall when the cat took over the house, or what life was like before he became a slave to the "Furry Empress," but he imagines he used to spend some time working as a playwright. His plays have been produced in Southern California and New York City, and have been described as "quirky and fun," and "containing a disappointingly small number of strong feline characters." His hobbies include reading, cleaning kitty litter from the soles of his shoes, painting, brushing cat hair from his sweaters, playing guitar, and desperately trying to escape. If you see him, please say hello, and please send help. All hail the Furry Empress.

BRINGING WORDS TO LIFE

Agnieszka Grochalska lives in Warsaw, Poland. She received her MFA in Graphic Arts in 2014. Along the way, she explored traditional painting, printmaking, and sculpting, but eventually dedicated her keen eye and steady hand to drawing precise, detailed art reminiscent of classical storybook illustrations. Her current work is predominantly in digital medium, and has been featured in group exhibitions both in Poland and abroad.

She enjoys travel and cultural exchanges with people from around the world, blending those experiences with the Slavic folklore of her homeland in her works. When she isn't drawing or traveling, you can find her exploring the worlds of fiction in books and story-driven games.

Agnieszka's portfolio can be found at agroshka.com.